"What's the proposition?"

"Are you agreeing?"

Tawny's even white teeth snapped together. "Like I have a choice?" she flashed back at him.

Rigid with resentment, Tawny looked at him, scanning the pure hard lines of his bronzed face. His eyes piercing with the weight of his intelligence, he wore an impenetrable mask of impassivity. He was incredibly handsome and incredibly unemotional. What the heck could the proposition be? She was a lowly chambermaid whom he believed to be a thief. In what possible way could she be of use to such a wealthy, powerful man? Even more to the point how could she put herself in such a man's power? Logic reminded her that as long as that unseen camera of his held an image of her apparently stealing she was in his power whether she liked it or not.

Marriage by Command

Three sisters wedlocked to the world's most powerful billionaires

A brand-new trilogy from USA TODAY bestselling author Lynne Graham!

The Blake heiresses have lived so long under the harsh rule of their father's iron fist, even the shackles of an arranged marriage seem like a reprieve—*at first!*

But they soon discover that they've jumped straight out of the frying pan…and into the fire. For their convenient husbands are men of the world—international, experienced and oh-so-devastatingly sexy!

Roccanti's Marriage Revenge

April—Zara's Story

Tricked!

Zara's very public engagement is hijacked by vengeful Italian billionaire Vitale Roccanti. The scandal they've created means there's no way left but down—*the aisle!*

A Deal at the Altar

May—Bee's story

Sold!

Bee is worth her weight in gold to Greek tycoon Sergios Demonides. But he needs her maternal skills rather than a trophy wife.

A Vow of Obligation

June—Tawny's story

Deceived!

Caught red-handed by her boss, Tawny is scandalized by Cazier's shocking proposal—a public engagement for her freedom!

Lynne Graham

A VOW OF OBLIGATION

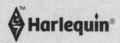

TORONTO NEW YORK LONDON
AMSTERDAM PARIS SYDNEY HAMBURG
STOCKHOLM ATHENS TOKYO MILAN MADRID
PRAGUE WARSAW BUDAPEST AUCKLAND

Recycling programs
for this product may
not exist in your area.

ISBN-13: 978-0-373-13073-3

A VOW OF OBLIGATION

Copyright © 2012 by Lynne Graham

www.Harlequin.com

Printed in U.S.A.

All about the author…
Lynne Graham

Born of Irish/Scottish parentage, **LYNNE GRAHAM** has lived in Northern Ireland all her life. She has one brother. She grew up in a seaside village and now lives in a country house surrounded by a woodland garden, which is wonderfully private.

Lynne first met her husband when she was fourteen. They married after she completed a degree at Edinburgh University. Lynne wrote her first book at fifteen and it was rejected everywhere. She started writing again when she was at home with her first child. It took several attempts before she sold her first book, and the delight of seeing that first book for sale in the local newsagents has never been forgotten.

Lynne always wanted a large family and has five children. Her eldest and her only natural child is in her 20s and a university graduate. Her other children, who are every bit as dear to her heart, are adopted: two from Sri Lanka and two from Guatemala. In Lynne's home, there is a rich and diverse cultural mix, which adds a whole extra dimension of interest and discovery to family life.

The family has two pets. Thomas, a very large and affectionate black cat, bosses the dog and hunts rabbits. The dog is Daisy, an adorable but not very bright white West Highland terrier, who loves being chased by the cat. At night, dog and cat sleep together in front of the kitchen stove.

Lynne loves gardening and cooking, collects everything from old toys to rock specimens and is crazy about every aspect of Christmas.

Other titles by Lynne Graham available in ebook

Harlequin Presents®

3061—A DEAL AT THE ALTAR *(Marriage by Command)*
3055—ROCCANTI'S MARRIAGE REVENGE
    (Marriage by Command)
3025—JEWEL IN HIS CROWN

CHAPTER ONE

'Were you seen coming up to my suite?' Navarre Cazier prompted in the Italian that came as naturally to him as the French of his homeland.

Tia pouted her famously sultry lips and in spite of her sophistication contrived to look remarkably young and naive as befitted one of the world's most acclaimed film stars. 'I slipped in through the side entrance—'

Navarre ditched his frown and smiled, for when she looked at him like that with her big blue eyes telegraphing embarrassed vulnerability he couldn't help it. 'It's you I'm concerned about. The paparazzi follow you everywhere—'

'Not here...' Tia Castelli declared, tossing her head so that a silken skein of honey-blonde hair rippled across her slim shoulders, her flawless face full of regret. 'We haven't got long though. Luke will be back at our hotel by three and I have to be there.'

At that reference to her notoriously volatile rock star husband, Navarre's lean, darkly handsome features hardened and his emerald-green eyes darkened.

Tia ran a manicured fingertip reprovingly below the implacable line of his shapely masculine mouth. 'Don't be like that, *caro mio*. This is my life, take me or leave me... and I couldn't bear it if you chose the second option!' she warned him in a sudden rush, her confident drawl splintering to betray the insecurity she hid from the world. 'I'm sorry, so sorry that it has to be like this between us!'

'It's OK,' Navarre told her soothingly although he was lying through his even white teeth as he said it. He loathed being a dirty little secret in her life but the alternative was to end their relationship and although he was remarkably strong-willed and stubborn, he had found himself quite unable to do that.

'And you're still bringing a partner with you for the awards ceremony, aren't you?' Tia checked anxiously. 'Luke is so incredibly suspicious of you.'

'Angelique Simonet, currently the toast of the Paris catwalk,' Navarre answered wryly.

'And she doesn't know about us?' the movie actress pressed worriedly.

'Of course not.'

'I know, I know…I'm sorry, I just have so much at stake!' Tia gasped strickenly. 'I couldn't stand to lose Luke!'

'You can trust me.' Navarre closed his arms round her slim body to comfort her. Her blue eyes glistened with the tears that came so easily to her and she was trembling with nerves. Navarre tried not to wonder what Luke Convery had been doing or saying to get her into such a state. Time and experience had taught him that it was better not to go there, better neither to know nor to enquire. He did not interfere in her marriage any more than she questioned his choice of lovers.

'I hate going so long without seeing you. It feels wrong,' she muttered heavily. 'But I've told so many lies I don't think that I could ever tell the truth.'

'It's not important,' Navarre told her with a gentleness

that would have astounded some of the women he had had in his life.

Navarre Cazier, the legendary French industrialist and billionaire, had the reputation of being a generous but distant lover to the beautiful women who passed through his bed. Yet even though he made no secret of his love of the single life, women remained infuriatingly keen to tell him that they loved him and to cling. Tia, however, occupied a category all of her own and he played by different rules with her. Accustomed as he was to independence from an early age, he was tough, self-reliant and unapologetically selfish but he always restrained that side of his nature with Tia and at least tried to accommodate her needs.

Later that afternoon when she had gone, Navarre was heading for the shower when his mobile buzzed beside the bed. Tia's distinctive perfume still hung in the air like a shamefaced marker of her recent presence. He would see her again soon but their next encounter would be in public and they would have to be circumspect for Luke Convery was a hothead, all too well aware of his gorgeous wife's chequered history of previous marriages and clandestine affairs. Tia's husband was always on the watch for signs that his wife's attention might be straying.

The call was from Angelique and Navarre's mood divebombed when he learned that his current lover was not, after all, coming to London to join him. Angelique had just been offered a television campaign by a famous cosmetics company and even Navarre could not fault her desire to make the most of such an opportunity.

Even so, it seemed to Navarre that life was cruelly conspiring to frustrate him. He *needed* Angelique this week and not only as a screen to protect Tia from the malicious rumours that had linked his name with hers on past occasions. He also had a difficult deal to close with the husband of a former lover, who had recently attempted to reanimate their affair. A woman on his arm and a supposedly serious relationship had been a non-negotiable necessity for Tia's peace of mind as well as good business practice in a difficult situation. *Merde alors,* what the hell was he going to do without a partner at this late stage in the game? Who could he possibly trust to play the game of a fake engagement and not attempt to take it further?

'Urgent—need 2 talk 2 you,' ran the text message that beeped on Tawny's mobile phone and she hurried downstairs to take her break, wondering what on earth was going on with her friend, Julie.

Julie worked as a receptionist in the same exclusive London hotel and, although the two young women had not known each other long, she had already proved herself to be a staunch and supportive friend. Her approachability had eased Tawny's first awkward days as a new employee when she had quickly discovered that as a chambermaid she was regarded as the lowest of the low by most of the other staff. She was grateful for Julie's company when their breaks coincided, but their friendship had gone well beyond that level, Tawny acknowledged with an appreciative smile. When, at short notice, Tawny had had to move out of her mother's home, Julie had helped her to find an affordable bedsit and had even offered her car to facilitate the move.

'I'm in trouble,' Julie, a very pretty brown-eyed blonde, said with a strong air of drama as Tawny joined her at a table in the corner of the dingy, almost empty staff room.

'What sort of trouble?'

Julie leant forwards to whisper conspiratorially, 'I slept with one of the guests.'

'But you'll be sacked if you've been caught out!' Tawny

exclaimed in dismay, brushing back the Titian red spiral curls clinging to her damp brow. Changing several beds in swift succession was tiring work and even though she was already halfway through a glass of cooling water she still felt overheated.

Julie rolled her eyes, unimpressed by the reminder. 'I haven't been caught out.'

Her porcelain-pale skin reddening, Tawny wished she had been more tactful, for she did not want Julie to think that she was judging her for her behaviour.

'Who was the guy?' she asked then, riven with curiosity for the blonde had not mentioned anyone, which could only mean that the relationship had been of sudden or short duration.

'It was Navarre Cazier.' Wearing a coy look of expectancy, Julie let the name hang there.

'Navarre Cazier?' Tawny was shocked by that familiar name.

She knew exactly who Julie was talking about because it was Tawny's responsibility to keep the penthouse suites on the top floor of the hotel in pristine order. The fabulously wealthy French industrialist stayed there at least twice a month and he always left her a massive tip. He didn't make unreasonable demands or leave his rooms in a mess either, which placed him head and shoulders above the other rich and invariably spoilt occupants of the most select accommodation offered by the hotel. She had only seen him once in the flesh, though, and at a distance, the giving of invisible service being one of the demands of her job. But after Julie had mentioned him several times in glowing terms Tawny had become curious enough to make the effort to catch a glimpse of him and had immediately understood why her friend was captivated. Navarre

Cazier was very tall, black-haired and even to her critical gaze, quite shockingly good-looking.

He also walked, talked and behaved like a god who ruled the world, Tawny recalled abstractedly. He had emerged from the lift at the head of a phalanx of awe-inspired minions clutching phones and struggling to follow reams of instructions hurled at them in two different languages. His sheer power of personality, volcanic energy and presence had had the brilliance of a searchlight in darkness. He had outshone everyone around him while administering a stinging rebuke to a cringing unfortunate who didn't react fast enough to an order. She had got the impression of a ferociously demanding male with a mind that functioned at the speed of a computer, a male, moreover, whose intrinsically high expectations were rarely satisfied by reality.

'As you know I've had my eye on Navarre for a while. He's absolutely gorgeous.' Julie sighed.

Navarre and Julie…*lovers?* A little pang of distaste assailed Tawny as she pulled free of her memories and returned to the present. It struck her as an incongruous pairing between two people who could have nothing in common, but Julie was extremely pretty and Tawny had seen enough of life to know that that was quite sufficient inducement for most men. Evidently the sophisticated French billionaire was not averse to the temptation of casual sex.

'So what's the problem?' Tawny asked in the strained silence that now stretched, resisting a tasteless urge to ask how the encounter had come about. 'Have you fallen pregnant or something?'

'Oh, don't be daft!' Julie fielded as if the very suggestion was a bad joke. 'But I did do something very stupid with him…'

Tawny was frowning. *'What?'* she pressed, unaccustomed to the other young woman being hesitant to talk about anything.

'I got so carried away I let him take a load of pictures of me posing in the nude. They're on his laptop!'

Tawny was aghast at the revelation and embarrassment sent hot colour winging into her cheeks. So, the French businessman liked to take photographs in the bedroom, Tawny thought with a helpless shudder of distaste. Navarre Cazier instantly sank below floor level in Tawny's fanciability stakes. *Ew!*

'What on earth made you agree to such a thing?' she questioned.

Julie clamped a tissue to her nose and Tawny was surprised to see tears swimming in her brown eyes, for Julie had always struck her as being rather a tough cookie. 'Julie?' she prompted more gently.

Julie grimaced in evident embarrassment, clearly fighting her distress. 'Surely you can guess why I agreed?' she countered in a voice choked with tears. 'I didn't want to seem like a prude…I wanted to please him. I hoped that if I was exciting enough he'd want to see me again. Rich guys get bored easily: you have to be willing to experiment to keep their interest. But I never heard from him again and now I feel sick at the idea of him still having those photos of me.'

Even though such reasoning made Tawny's heart sink she understood it perfectly. Once upon a time her mother, Susan, had been equally keen to impress a rich man. In Susan's case the man had been her boss and their subsequent secret affair had continued on and off for years before finally running aground over the pregnancy that produced Tawny and her mother's lowering discovery that she was far from being her lover's only extra-marital interest.

'Ask him to delete the photographs,' Tawny suggested stiffly, feeling more than a little out of her depth with the subject but naturally sympathetic towards her friend's disillusionment. She knew how deeply hurt her mother had been to ultimately discover that her long-term lover didn't consider her worthy of a more permanent or public relationship. But after only one night of intimacy, she felt that Julie would recover rather more easily from the betrayal than Tawny's mother had.

'I asked him to delete them soon after he arrived yesterday. He flatly refused.'

Tawny was stumped by that frank admission. 'Well er...'

'But all I would need is five minutes with his laptop to take care of it for myself,' Julie told her in an urgent undertone.

Tawny was unsurprised by the claim for she had heard that Julie was skilled in IT and often the first port of call when the office staff got into a snit with a computer. 'He's hardly going to give you access to his laptop,' she pointed out wryly.

'No, but if I could get hold of his laptop, what harm would it do for me to deal with the problem right there and then?'

Tawny studied the other woman fixedly. 'Are you seriously planning to try and steal the guy's laptop?'

'I just want to borrow it for five minutes and, as I don't have access to his suite and you *do,* I was hoping that you would do it for me.'

Tawny fell back in her seat, pale blue eyes wide with disbelief as she stared back at the other woman in dismay. 'You've got to be joking...'

'There would be no risk. I'd tell you when he was out, you could go in and I could rush upstairs and wait next door in the storage room for you to bring the laptop out to me. Five minutes, that's all it would take for me to delete those photos. You'll replace it in his room and he'll never know what happened to them!' Julie argued forcefully. *'Please,* Tawny…it would mean so much to me. Haven't you ever done something you regret?'

'I'd like to help you but I can't do something illegal,' Tawny protested, pulling a face in the tense silence. 'That laptop is his personal property and interfering with it would be a criminal offence—'

'He's never going to know that anyone's even touched it! That possibility won't even occur to him,' Julie argued vehemently. 'Please, Tawny. You're the only person who can help me.'

'I couldn't— There's just no way I could do something like that,' Tawny muttered uneasily. 'I'm sorry.'

Julie touched her hand to regain her attention. 'We haven't got much time—he'll be checking out again the day after tomorrow. I'll talk to you again at lunch time before you finish your shift.'

'I won't change my mind,' Tawny warned, compressing her soft full mouth in discomfiture.

'Think it over—it's a foolproof plan,' Julie insisted as she stood up, lowering her voice even more to add huskily, 'And if it would make a difference, I'm willing to pay you to take that risk for me—'

'Pay me?' Tawny was very much taken aback by that offer.

'What else can I do? You're my only hope in this situation,' Julie reasoned plaintively. 'If a bit of money would make you feel better about doing this, of course I'm going to suggest it. I know how desperate you are to help your grandmother out.'

'Look, money's got nothing to do with the way I feel. Just leave it out of this,' Tawny urged in considerable embarrassment. 'If I was in a position to help out, it wouldn't cost you a penny.'

Tawny returned to work with her thoughts in turmoil. Navarre Cazier, handsome, rich and privileged though he was, had cruelly used and abused Julie's trust. Another rich four-letter word of a man was grinding an ordinary woman down. But that unfortunately was life, wasn't it? The rich lived by different rules and enjoyed enormous power and influence. Hadn't her own father taught her that? He had dumped her mother when she refused to have a termination and had paid her a legal pittance to raise his unwanted child to adulthood. There had been no extras in Tawny's childhood and not much love on offer either from a mother who had bitterly regretted her decision to have her baby and a father who did not even pretend an interest in his illegitimate daughter. To be fair, her mother *had* paid a high price for choosing to bring her child into the world. Not only had her lover ditched her, but she had also found it impossible to continue her career.

Tawny suppressed those unproductive reflections and thought worriedly about Julie instead. She felt really bad about having refused to help her friend. Julie had been very good to her and had never asked her for anything in return. But why the heck had Julie offered her a financial bribe to get hold of that laptop? She was deeply embarrassed that Julie should be so aware of her financial constraints and regretted her honesty on that topic.

In truth, Tawny only worked at the hotel to earn enough money to ensure that her grandmother could continue to pay the rent on her tiny apartment in a private retirement village. Celestine, devastated by the combined death of her beloved husband and, with him, the loss of her marital home, had, against all the odds, contrived to make a happy new life and friends in the village, and there was little that Tawny would not do to safeguard the old lady's tenure there. Unfortunately rising costs had quickly outstripped her grandmother's ability to pay her bills. Tawny, having taken charge of Celestine's financial affairs, had chosen to quietly supplement her grandmother's income without her knowledge, which was why she was currently working as a chambermaid. Prior to the crisis in the old lady's finances, Tawny had made her living by illustrating children's books and designing greeting cards, but sadly there was insufficient work in that field during an economic crisis to stretch to shoring up Celestine's income as well as covering Tawny's own living costs. Now Tawny's artistic projects took up evenings and weekends instead.

But, regardless of that situation, wasn't it rather insulting that a friend should offer to *pay* you to do something for them? Tawny reasoned uneasily. On the other hand, wasn't that inappropriate suggestion merely proof of Julie's desperate need for her assistance?

Would it be so very bad of her to do what she could to help Julie delete those distasteful photos? While Tawny could not even imagine trusting a man enough to take pictures of her naked body, she could understand Julie's cringing reluctance to continue featuring in some sort of X-rated scalp gallery on the guy's laptop. That was a downright demeaning and extremely offensive prospect to have to live with. Would he let other men access those pictures? Tawny grimaced in disgust, incensed that a guy she had believed was attractive could turn out to be such a creep.

'All right, I'll have a go at getting hold of it for you,' she told Julie at lunchtime.

Her friend's face lit up immediately and a wide smile of satisfaction formed on her lips. 'I'll make sure you don't regret it!'

Tawny was unconvinced by that assurance but concealed her fear of the consequences, feeling that she ought to be more courageous. She wore colourful vintage clothing, held strong opinions and her ultimate ambition was to become a cartoonist with a strip of her own in a magazine or newspaper. In short she liked to think of herself as an individual rather than a follower. But sometimes, she suspected that deep down inside she was more of a conventional person than she liked to admit because she longed for a supportive family and had never broken the law by even the smallest margin.

'We'll do it this afternoon. As soon as his room is empty, if there's no sign of him having the laptop with him I'll ring up and you can go straight in and get it. Just leave it in the storage room. I'll be there within two minutes,' Julie told her eagerly.

'You're absolutely sure that you want to do this?' Tawny pressed worriedly. 'Perhaps you should speak to him again. If we get caught—'

'We're not going to get caught!' Julie declared with cutting conviction. 'Stop making such a fuss.'

Tawny went pink, assumed that Julie's outburst was the result of nervous tension and fell silent, but that tart response had set her own fiery temper on edge.

'Just go back to work and act normally,' Julie advised, shooting Tawny an apologetic look. 'I'll call you.'

Tawny returned with relief to changing beds, vacuuming and scrubbing bathrooms. She kept so busy she didn't allow herself to think about that call coming and yet on some level she was on hyper alert for when she heard the faint ping of the lift doors opening down the corridor she jumped almost a foot in the air. Julie's call telling her that his assistant had just left and the room was empty came barely a minute after that. Her heart beating very fast, Tawny sped down the passage with her trolley. Arming herself with a change of bedding as an excuse she used her pass key to let herself into Navarre Cazier's spacious suite. She set the fresh sheets down on the arm of a sofa as her eyes did a frantic sweep of the reception room and zoomed in on the laptop sitting conveniently on the table by the window. Although it was the work of a moment to cross the room, unplug the computer from its charger and tuck it below her arm, her skin dampened with perspiration and her stomach churned. Turning on her heel, she literally raced back to the exit door, eager to hand over the laptop to Julie and refusing to even think about having to sneak back in again to return it.

Without the slightest warning, however, there was a click and the door of the suite snapped open. Eyes huge with fright, Tawny clutched the laptop and froze into stillness. Navarre Cazier appeared and it was not a good time for her to realise that he was much bigger than he had seemed at a distance. He towered over her five and a half feet by well over six inches, his shoulders wide as axe handles in his formal dark suit. He was much more of an athlete in build than the average businessman. She clashed in dismay with frowning chartreuse-green eyes, startlingly bright and unexpected in that olive-skinned face. Close up he was quite breathtakingly handsome.

'Is that my laptop?' he asked immediately, his attention flying beyond her to the empty table. 'Has there been an accident? What are you doing with it?'

'I…I er…' Her heart was beating so fast it felt as if it

were thumping at the foot of her throat and her mind was a punishing blank.

There was a burst of French from behind him and he moved deeper into the room to make way for the bodyguards that accompanied him virtually everywhere he went.

'I will call the police, Navarre,' his security chief, Jacques, a well-built older man, said decisively in French.

'No, no...no need to bring the police in!' Tawny exclaimed, now ready to kick herself for not having grabbed at the excuse that she had accidentally knocked the laptop off the table while cleaning.

'You speak French?' Navarre studied her with growing disquiet, taking in the uniform of blue tunic and trousers she wore with flat heels. Evidently she worked for the hotel in a menial capacity: there was an unattended cleaning trolley parked directly outside the suite. Of medium height and slender build, she had a delicate pointed face dominated by pale blue eyes the colour of an Alpine glacier set in porcelain-perfect skin, the combination enlivened by a mop of vivid auburn curls escaping from a ponytail. Navarre had always liked redheads and her hair was as bright as a tropical sunset.

'My grandmother is French,' Tawny muttered, deciding that honesty might now be her only hope of escaping a criminal charge.

If she spoke fluent French the potential for damage was even greater, Navarre reckoned furiously. How long had she had his laptop for? He had been out for an hour. Unfortunately it would only take minutes for her to copy the hard drive, gaining access not only to highly confidential business negotiations but also to even more personal and theoretically damaging emails. How many indiscreet emails of Tia's might she have seen? He was appalled by the breach in his security. 'What are you doing with my laptop?'

Tawny lifted her chin. 'I'm willing to explain but I don't think you'll want an audience while we have that conversation,' she dared.

His strong jawline clenched at that impertinent challenge as he read the name on her badge. Tawny Baxter, an apt label for a woman with such spectacular hair. 'There is no reason why you should not speak in front of my security staff,' he replied impatiently.

'Julie—the receptionist you spent the night with on your last visit,' Tawny specified curtly, surrendering the laptop as one of his security team put out his hands to reclaim the item. 'Julie just wants the photos you took of her posing wiped from your laptop.'

His ebony brows drawing together, Navarre subjected her to an incredulous scrutiny while absently noting the full pouting curve of her pink lips. She was in possession of what had to be the most temptingly sultry mouth he had ever seen on a woman. Exasperated by that abstracted thought, he straightened his broad shoulders and declared, 'I have never spent the night with a receptionist in this hotel. What kind of a scam are you trying to pull?'

'Don't waste your breath on this dialogue, Navarre. Let me contact the police,' the older man urged impatiently.

'Her name is Julie Chivers, she works on reception and right now she's waiting in the storage room next door for the laptop,' Tawny extended in a feverish rush. 'All she wants is to delete the photos you took of her!'

With an almost imperceptible movement of his arrogant dark head, Navarre directed Jacques to check out that location and the older man ducked back out of the room. Tawny sucked in a lungful of air and tilted her chin. 'Why wouldn't you wipe the photos when Julie asked you to?'

'I have no idea what you're talking about,' he countered with a chilly gravity that sank like an icicle deep into her tender flesh. 'There was no night with a receptionist, no photos. Ditch the silly story. What have you done with my laptop?'

'Absolutely nothing. I'd only just lifted it when you appeared,' Tawny replied tightly, wondering why he was still lying and eagerly watching the door for Julie's appearance. She was sure that once he recognised her friend as a former lover there would be no more talk of calling the police. But didn't he even recognise Julie's name? It occurred to her that she never wanted to become intimate with a man who didn't care enough even to take note of her name.

'It's unfortunate for you that I came back unexpectedly,' Navarre shot back at her, wholly unconvinced by her plea.

Of course she would try to tell him that she had not had enough time to do any real damage. But he was too conscious that she could have copied his hard drive within minutes and might even be concealing a flash drive beneath her clothing. He was in the act of doubting that the police would agree to have her strip-searched for the sake of his security and peace of mind so his attention quite naturally rested on her slender coltish shape.

She had a gloriously tiny waist. He could not help wondering if the skin of her body was as pearly and perfect as that of her face. When almost every woman he knew practically bathed in fake tan it was a novelty to see a woman so pale he could see the faint tracery of blue veins beneath her skin. Indeed the more he studied her, the more aware he became of her unusual delicate beauty and the tightening fullness at his groin was his natural masculine reaction to her allure. She had that leggy pure-bred look but those big pale eyes and that wickedly suggestive mouth etched buckets of raw sex appeal into her fragile features. That she could look that good even without make-up was unparalleled in his experience of her sex. In the right clothes with that amazing hair loose she would probably be a complete knockout. What a shame she was a humble chambermaid about to be charged with petty theft, he reflected impatiently, returning his thoughts to reality while marvelling at the detour into fantasy that they had briefly and bizarrely taken.

Jacques reappeared and shook his head in response to his employer's enquiring glance. Something akin to panic gripped Tawny. Evidently Julie wasn't still in the storage room ready and able to make an explanation. Until that instant Tawny had not appreciated just how much she had been depending on her friend coming through that door and immediately sorting out the misunderstanding.

'Julie must have heard you come back and she's gone back downstairs to Reception,' Tawny reasoned in dismay.

'I'm calling the police,' Navarre breathed, turning to lift the phone.

'No, let me call Reception and ask Julie to come up and explain first,' Tawny urged in a frantic rush. '*Please*, Mr Cazier!'

For a split second Navarre scanned her pleading eyes, marvelling at their rare colour, and then he swept up the phone and, while she held her breath in fear and watched, he stabbed the button for Reception and requested her friend by name.

Colour slowly returning to her drawn cheeks, Tawny drew in a tremulous breath. 'I'm not lying to you, I swear I'm not... I didn't even get the chance to open your laptop—'

'Naturally you will say that,' Navarre derided. 'You

could well have been in the act of returning it to the room when I surprised you—'

'But I *wasn't!*' Tawny exclaimed in horror when she registered the depth of his suspicion. 'I had only just lifted it when you returned. I'm telling you the truth!'

'That I had some kinky one-night stand with a camera and a receptionist?' Navarre queried with stinging scorn. 'Do I strike you as that desperate for entertainment in London?'

Suffering her very first moment of doubt as to his guilt in that quarter, Tawny shrugged a slight shoulder in an awkward gesture while her heart sank at the possibility that she could be wrong. 'How would I know? You're a guest here. I know nothing about you aside of what my friend told me.'

'Your friend lied to you,' Navarre declared.

After a tense two minutes of complete silence a soft knock sounded on the door and Julie entered, looking unusually meek. 'How can I help you, Mr Cazier?'

'*Julie...*' Tawny interposed, leaping straight into speech. 'I want you to explain about you asking me to take the laptop so that we can get this all sorted out—'

'What about the laptop? Take *whose* laptop?' Julie enquired sharply, widening her brown eyes in apparent confusion and annoyance. 'What the hell are you trying to accuse me of doing?'

In receipt of that aggressive comeback, Tawny was bewildered. She could feel the blood draining from her cheeks in shock and the sick churning in the pit of her stomach started up afresh. 'Julie, please explain…look, what's going on here? You and Mr Cazier know each other—'

Julie's brow pleated. 'If you mean by that that Mr Cazier is a regular and much respected guest here—'

'You told me that he took photos of you—'

'I have no idea what you're talking about. Photos? I'm sorry about this, Mr Cazier. Possibly this member of staff has been drinking or something because she's talking nonsense. I should call the penthouse manager to deal with this situation.'

'Thank you, Miss Chivers, but that won't be necessary. You may leave,' Navarre cut in with clear impatience. 'I've heard quite enough.'

Navarre motioned his security chief back to his side with the movement of one finger and addressed the older man in an undertone.

In disbelief, Tawny watched her erstwhile friend leave the suite with her head held high. Julie had lied. Julie had actually pretended not to know her on a personal basis. Her friend had *lied,* turned her back on Tawny and let her take the fall for attempted theft. Tawny was not only stunned by that betrayal, but also no longer convinced that Julie had ever spent the night with Navarre Cazier. But if that suspicion was true, why had Julie told her that convoluted story about the nude photography session? Why else would Julie have wanted access to the billionaire's laptop? What had she wanted to find out from it and why?

As Tawny turned white and swayed Navarre thought she might be about to faint. Instead, demonstrating a surprising amount of inner strength for so young a woman, she leant back against the wall for support and breathed in slow and deep to steady herself. Even so, he recognised an attack of gut-deep fear when he saw one but he had not the slightest pity for her. Navarre always hit back hard against those who tried to injure him. At the same time, however, he also reasoned at the speed of light, an ability that had dug him out of some very tight corners while growing up.

If he called the police, what recompense would he receive for the possible crime committed against him? There would be no guarantee that the maid would be punished and even if this was not a first offence she would be released, possibly even to take advantage of selling a copy of his hard drive to either his business competitors or the paparazzi, who had long sought proof of the precise nature of his relationship with Tia. Either prospect promised far reaching repercussions, not just to his extensive business empire, but even more importantly to Tia, her marriage and her reputation. He owed Tia his protection, he reflected grimly. But it might already be too late to prevent revealing private correspondence entering the public domain.

On the other hand, if he were to prevent the maid from contacting anyone to pass on confidential information for at least the next seven days, he could considerably minimise the risks to all concerned. Granted a week's grace the business deal with the Coulter Centax Corporation, CCC, could be tied up and, should his fear with regard to the emails prove correct, Tia's world-class PR advisors would have the chance to practise damage limitation on her behalf. In the event of the worst-case scenario isolating the maid was the most effective action he could currently take.

And, even more to the point, if he was forced to keep the maid around he might well be able to make use of her presence, Navarre decided thoughtfully. She was young and beautiful. And, crucially, he already knew that her loyalty could be bought. Why should he not pay her to fill the role that presently stood empty? With a movement of his hand he dismissed Jacques and his companion. The older man left the suite with clear reluctance.

Tawny gazed back at Navarre, her triangular face taut with strain. 'I really wasn't trying to steal from you—'

'The camera recording in here won't lie,' Navarre murmured without any expression at all, lush black lashes low over intent green eyes.

'There's a camera operating in here?' Tawny exclaimed in horror, immediately recognising that if there was he would have unquestionable proof of her entering the suite and taking his laptop.

'My protection team set up a camera as a standard safeguard wherever I'm staying,' Navarre stated smooth as glass. 'It means that I will have pictorial evidence of your attempt to steal from me.'

Her narrow shoulders slumped and her face fell. Shame gutted her for, whatever her motivation had been, theft was theft and neither the police nor a judge would distinguish between what she had believed she was doing and a crime. She marvelled that she had foolishly got herself into such a predicament. Caught red-handed as she had been, it no longer seemed a good idea to continue to insist that she had not been stealing. 'Yes…'

'Having you sacked and arrested, however, will be of no advantage to me,' Navarre Cazier asserted and she glanced up in surprise. 'But if you were to accept my terms in the proposition I am about to make you, I will not contact the police and in addition I will pay you for your time.'

Genuinely stunned by the content of that speech, Tawny lifted her head and speared him with an ice-blue look of scorn. 'Pay me for my time? I'm not that kind of girl—'

Navarre laughed out loud, grim amusement lightening the gravity on his face as her eyes flashed and her chin came up in challenge. 'My proposition doesn't entail taking your clothes off or, indeed, doing anything of an illegal or sexual nature,' he extended very drily. 'Make your mind up—this is very much your decision. Do I call the police or are you going to be sensible and reach for the lifebelt I'm offering?'

CHAPTER TWO

TAWNY straightened her shoulders. Her mind was in a fog torn between panic and irrational hope while she tried to work out if the exclusion of either illegal or sexual acts would offer her sufficient protection. 'You'll have to tell me first what grabbing the lifebelt would entail.'

'*Rien à faire*…nothing doing. I can't trust you with that information until I know that I have your agreement,' Navarre Cazier fielded without hesitation.

'I can't agree to something when I don't know what it is…you can't expect that.'

His stunning eyes narrowed to biting chips of emerald. '*Merde alors*…I'm the party in the position of power here. I can ask whatever I like. After all, you have the right of refusal.'

'I don't want to be accused of theft. I don't want a police record,' Tawny admitted through gritted teeth of resentment. 'I am not a thief, Mr Cazier—'

Navarre Cazier expelled his breath in a weary sigh that suggested he was not convinced of that claim. Tawny went red and her slender hands closed into fists. She was in a daze of desperation, trapped and fighting a dangerous urge to lose her temper. 'This proposition—would I be able to accept it and keep my job on here?' she pressed.

'Not unless the hotel was prepared to allow you a leave of absence of at least two weeks.'

'I don't have that kind of flexibility,' Tawny said heavily.

'But I did say that I'd pay you for your time,' Navarre reminded her drily.

That salient reminder, when Tawny was worrying about how the loss of her job would impact on her ability to pay her grandmother's mortgage, was timely. 'What's the proposition?'

'Are you agreeing?'

Her even white teeth snapped together. 'Like I have a choice?' she flashed back at him. 'Yes. Assuming there's nothing illegal, sexual or offensive about what you're asking me to do.'

'How would I know what you find offensive? Give me a final answer. Right now you're wasting my valuable time.'

Rigid with resentment, Tawny looked at him, scanning the pure hard lines of his bronzed face. His eyes piercing with the weight of his intelligence, he wore an impenetrable mask of impassivity. He was incredibly handsome and incredibly unemotional. What could the proposition be? She was a lowly chambermaid whom he believed to be a thief. In what possible way could she be of use to such a wealthy, powerful man? Even more to the point, how could she put herself in such a man's power? Logic reminded her that as long as that unseen camera of his held an image of her apparently stealing she was in his power whether she liked it or not.

'How much would you pay me?' Tawny prompted drymouthed, her face burning as she tried to weigh up her single option.

Realising that they were finally dealing in business

terms, Navarre's emerald-green gaze glittered with renewed energy. He estimated what she most probably earned in a year and doubled it in the sum he came back to her with. Although it went against the grain with him to reward criminal behaviour, he was aware that if she was to lose her job in meeting his demands he had to make it worth her financial while. She went pale, her eyes widening in shock, and in the same moment he knew he had her exactly where he wanted her. Everyone had their price and he had, it seemed, accurately assessed hers.

That amount of money would cover any future period of unemployment she might suffer as well as her grandmother's mortgage for the rest of the year and more, Tawny registered in wonderment. But the truth that he had her pinned between a rock and a hard place was still a bitter pill to swallow. She would accept the money, but then any alternative was better than being arrested and charged with theft. She jerked her chin in affirmation. 'I'll do whatever it is as long as you promise to wipe that camera once it's done.'

'And I will accept that arrangement as long as you sign a confidentiality agreement, guaranteeing not to discuss anything you see or hear while you're in my company.'

'No problem. I'm not a chatterbox,' Tawny traded flatly. 'May I return to work now?'

Navarre dealt her an impatient look. 'I'm afraid not. You can't leave this hotel room without an escort. I want to be sure that any intel you may have gleaned from my laptop stays within these four walls.'

It finally dawned on Tawny that he had to have some highly sensitive information on that laptop when he was prepared to go to such lengths to protect it from the rest of the world. A knock sounded on the door and Navarre strode across the room, his tall, well-built body emanating aggressive male power, to pull it open. Tawny went pale when she saw the penthouse manager, Lesley Morgan, in the doorway.

'Excuse me, Mr Cazier. Reception mentioned that there might be a problem—'

'There is not a problem.'

'Tawny?' Lesley queried quietly. 'I'm sure you must have work to take care of—'

'Tawny is resigning from her job, effective immediately,' Navarre Cazier slotted in without hesitation.

Across the room Tawny went rigid but she neither confirmed nor protested his declaration. In receipt of a wildly curious glance from the attractive brunette, Tawny flushed uncomfortably. So, she was going to be unemployed while she fulfilled his mysterious mission. It was an obvious first step. Whatever he wanted from her she could hardly continue to work a daily shift at the hotel at the same time. On the other hand, she would be virtually unemployable with a criminal record for theft hanging over her head, and, if she could emerge from the agreement with the French industrialist with her good name still intact, losing her current job would be a worthwhile sacrifice.

'There are certain formalities to be taken care of in the case of termination of employment,' Lesley replied with an apologetic compression of her lips.

'Which my staff will deal with on Tawny's behalf,' Navarre retorted in a tone of finality.

Beneath Tawny's bemused gaze, the penthouse manager took her leave. Navarre left Tawny hovering in the centre of the carpet while he made a brisk phone call to an employee to instruct her to organise appointments for him. A frown divided Tawny's fine brows when she heard him mention her name. He spoke in French too fast for her to follow to a couple of other people and then finally tossed the phone down. A knock sounded on the door.

'Answer that,' Navarre told her.

'Say please,' Tawny specified, bravely challenging him. 'You may be paying me but you can still be polite.'

Navarre stiffened in disbelief. 'I have excellent manners.'

'No, you don't...I've seen you operating with your staff,' Tawny countered with a suggestive wince. 'It's all, *do* this, *do* that...why haven't you done it already? Please and thank you don't figure —'

'Open the damn door!' Navarre raked at her, out of all patience.

'You're not just rude, you're a bully,' Tawny declared, stalking over to the door to tug it open with a twist of a slender hand.

'Don't answer me back like that,' Navarre warned her as his security chief walked in and, having caught that last exchange, directed an astonished look of curiosity at his employer.

'You're far too tempting a target,' Tawny warned him.

Icy green eyes caught her amused gaze and chilled her. 'Control the temptation. If you can't do as you're told you're of no use to me at all.'

'Is that the sound of a whip cracking over my head?' Tawny looked skyward.

'Do you hear anyone laughing?' Navarre derided.

'You've got your staff too scared.'

'Jacques, take Tawny to collect her belongings and bring her back up without giving her the chance to talk to anyone,' Navarre instructed.

'Men aren't allowed in the female locker room,' Tawny told him gently.

'I will ask Elise to join us.' Jacques unfurled his phone.

Navarre studied Tawny, far from impervious to the amusement glimmering in her pale eyes combined with the voluptuous pout of her sexy mouth. Desire, sudden and piercing as a blade, gripped him. All of a sudden as he met those eyes he was picturing her on a bed with rumpled sheets, hair fanned out in a wild colourful torrent of curls, that pale slender body displayed for his pleasure. His teeth clenched on the shot of stark hunger that evocative image released. He was consoled by the near certainty that she would give him that pleasure before their association ended, for no woman had ever denied him.

Gazing back at Navarre Cazier, Tawny momentarily felt as though someone had, without the smallest warning, dropped her off the side of a cliff. Her body felt as if it had gone into panic mode, her heartbeat thundering far too fast, her mouth suddenly dry, her nipples tight and swollen, an excited fluttering low in her belly. And just as quickly Tawny realised what was *really* happening to her and she tore her attention guiltily from him, colour burning over her cheekbones at her uncontrollable reaction to all that male testosterone in the air. It was desire he had awakened, not fear. Yes, he was gorgeous, but under no circumstances was she going to go there.

Rich, handsome men didn't attract her. Her mother and her sisters' experiences had taught Tawny not to crave wealth and status for the sake of it, for neither brought lasting happiness. Her father, a noted hotelier, was rich and miserable and, according to her older half-sisters, Bee and Zara, he was always pleading dissatisfaction with his life or latest business deal. Nothing was ever enough for Monty Blake. Bee and Zara might also be married to wealthy men, but they were both very much in love with their husbands. At the end of the day love was all that really mattered, Tawny reflected thoughtfully, and substituting sex for love and hoping it would bridge the gap didn't work.

That was why Tawny didn't sleep around. She had grown up with her mother's bitterness over a sexual affair that had never amounted to anything more. She had also seen too many friends hurt by their efforts to found a lasting relationship on a basis of casual sex. She wanted more commitment before she risked her heart; she had always wanted and demanded *more*. That was the main reason why she had avoided the advances of the wealthy men introduced to her by her matchmaking sisters, both of whom had married 'well' in her mother's parlance. What could she possibly have in common with such men with their flash lives in which only materialistic success truly mattered? She had no wish to end up with a vain, shallow and selfish man like her father, who was solely interested in her for her looks.

'Are you going to tell me what this proposition entails?' Tawny prompted in the simmering silence.

'I want you to pretend to be my fiancée,' Navarre spelt out grimly.

Her eyes widened to their fullest, for that had to be almost the very last thing she might have expected. 'But why?' she exclaimed.

'You have no need of that information,' Navarre fielded drily.

'But you must know loads of women who would—'

'Perhaps I prefer to pay. Think of yourself as a professional escort. I'll be buying you a new wardrobe to wear while you're with me. When this is over you get to keep the clothes, but not the jewellery,' he specified.

No expense spared, she thought in growing bewilderment. She had read about him in the newspapers, for he made regular appearances in the gossip columns. He had a penchant for incredibly beautiful supermodels and the reputation of being a legendary lover, but none of the ladies in his life seemed to last very long. 'Nobody's going to believe you're engaged to someone as ordinary as me,' she told him baldly.

'Ce fut le coup de foudre...' It was love at first sight French-style, he was telling her with sardonic cool. 'And nobody will be surprised when the relationship quickly bites the dust again.'

Well, she could certainly agree with that final forecast, but she reckoned that he had to be desperate to be considering her for such a role. How on earth would she ever be able to compare to the glamorous model types he usually had on his arm? Jacques ushered a statuesque blonde in a dark trouser suit into the room. 'Elise will escort you down to the locker room,' he explained.

'So you're a bodyguard,' Tawny remarked in French as the two women waited in the lift.

'I'm usually the driver,' Elise admitted.

'What's Mr Cazier like to work for?'

'Tough but fair and I get to travel,' Elise told her with satisfaction.

Elise hovered nearby while Tawny changed out of her uniform into her own clothes and cleared her locker. The Frenchwoman's mobile phone rang and she dug it out, glancing awkwardly at Tawny, who was busily packing a carrier bag full of belongings before moving to the other side of the room to talk in a low-pitched voice. That it was a man Elise cared about at the other end of the line was obvious, and Tawny reckoned that at that instant she could have smuggled an elephant past the Frenchwoman without attracting her attention.

'What's going on?' another voice enquired tautly of Tawny.

Tawny glanced up and focused on Julie, who stood only a couple of feet away from her. 'I'm quitting my job.'

'I heard that but why didn't he report you?'

Tawny shrugged non-committally. 'You didn't spent the night with him, did you? What's the real story?'

'A journalist offered me a lot of money to dig out some personal information for him. Accessing Cazier's laptop was worth a try. I've got credit cards to clear,' Julie admitted calmly, shockingly unembarrassed at having her lies exposed.

'Mademoiselle Baxter?' Elise queried anxiously, her attention suddenly closely trained on the two women.

Tawny lifted her laden bags and walked away without another word or look. So much for friendship! She was furious but also very hurt by her former friend's treachery. She had liked Julie, she had automatically trusted her, but she could now see her whole relationship with the other woman in quite a different light. It was likely that Julie had deliberately targeted her once she realised that Tawny would be the new maid in charge of Navarre Cazier's usual suite. Having befriended Tawny and put her under obligation by helping her to move into her bedsit, Julie had then conned the younger woman into trying to take Navarre's laptop. What a stupid, trusting fool Tawny now felt like! How could she have been dumb enough to swallow that improbable tale of sex and compromising photos? Julie had known exactly which buttons to press to engage Tawny's sympathies and it would have worked a treat had Navarre Cazier not returned unexpectedly to catch her in the act.

'You have an appointment with a stylist,' Navarre informed Tawny when she reappeared in his suite and set down her bags.

'Where?'

He named a famous department store. He scanned the jeans and checked shirt she wore with faded blue plimsolls and his wide sensual mouth twisted, for in such casual clothing she looked little older than a teenager. 'What age are you?'

'Twenty-three…you?'

'Thirty.'

'Speak French,' he urged.

'I'm a little rusty. I only get to see my grandmother about once a month now,' Tawny told him.

'Give me your mobile phone,' he instructed.

'My phone?' Tawny exclaimed in dismay.

'I can't trust you with access to a phone when I need to ensure that you don't pass information to anyone,' he retorted levelly and extended a slim brown hand. 'Your phone, please…'

The silence simmered. Tawny worried at her lower lip, reckoned that she could not fault his reasoning and reluctantly dug her phone out of her pocket. 'You're not allowed to go through it. There's private stuff on there.'

'Just like my laptop,' Navarre quipped with a hard look, watching her redden and marvelling that she could still blush so easily.

He ushered her out of the suite and into the lift. She leant back against the wall.

'Don't slouch,' he told her immediately.

With an exaggerated sigh, Tawny straightened. 'We mix like oil and water.'

'We only have to impress as a couple in company. Practise looking adoring,' Navarre advised witheringly.

Tawny wrinkled her nose. 'That's not really my style—'

'*Try,*' he told her.

She preceded him out into the foyer, striving not to notice the heads craning at the reception desk to follow their progress out of the hotel. A limousine was waiting by the kerb and she climbed in, noting Elise's neat blonde head behind the steering wheel.

'Tell me about yourself…a potted history,' Navarre instructed.

'I'm an only child although I have two half-sisters through my father's two marriages. He didn't marry my mother, though, and he has never been involved in my life. I got my degree at art college and for a couple of years managed to make a living designing greeting cards. Unfortunately that wasn't lucrative enough to pay the bills and I signed up as a maid so that I would have a regular wage coming in,' she told him grudgingly. 'I want to be a cartoonist but so far I haven't managed to sell a single cartoon.'

'A cartoonist,' Navarre repeated, his interest caught by that unexpected ambition.

'What about you? Were you born rich?'

'No. I grew up in the back streets of Paris but I acquired a first-class degree at the Sorbonne. I was an investment banker until I became interested in telecommunications and set up my first business.'

'Parents?' she pressed.

His face tensed. 'I was a foster child and lived in many homes. I have no relatives that I acknowledge.'

'I know how we can tell people we met,' Tawny said with a playful light in her eyes. 'I was changing your bed *when*—'

Navarre was not amused by the suggestion but his attention lingered on her astonishingly vivid little face in which every expression was easily read. 'I don't think we need to admit that you were working as a hotel maid.'

'Honesty is always the best policy.'

'Says the woman whom I caught thieving.'

Her face froze as though he had slapped her, reality biting again. 'I wasn't thieving,' she muttered tightly.

'It really doesn't matter as long as you keep your light fingers strictly to your own belongings while you're with me,' Navarre responded drily. 'I hope the desire to steal is an impulse that you can resist as we will be mingling with some very wealthy people.'

Mortified by the comment, Tawny bent her bright head. 'Yes, you don't have to worry on that score.'

While Navarre took a comfortable seat in a private room in the store, Tawny was ushered off to try on evening gowns, and each one seemed more elaborate than the last. When the selection had been reduced to two she was propelled out to the waiting area, where Navarre was perusing the financial papers, for a second opinion.

'That's too old for her,' he commented of the purple ball gown that she felt would not have looked out of place on Marie Antoinette.

When she walked out in the grey lace that fitted like a glove to below hip line before flaring out in a romantic arc of fullness round her knees, he actually set his newspaper down, the better to view her slender, shapely figure. *'Sensationnel,'* he declared with crowd-pleasing enthusiasm while his shrewd green eyes scanned her with as much emotion as a wooden clothes horse might have inspired.

Yet for all that lack of feeling they were such unexpectedly beautiful eyes, she reflected helplessly, as cool and mysterious as the depths of the sea, set in that strong handsome face. Bemused by the unusually fanciful thought, Tawny was whisked back into the spacious changing room where two assistants were hanging up outfits for the stylist to choose from. There were trousers, skirts, dresses, tops and jackets as well as lingerie and a large selection of shoes and accessories. Every item was designer and classic and nothing was colourful enough or edgy enough to appeal to her personal taste. She would only be in the role of fake fiancée for a maximum of two weeks, she reminded herself with relief. Could such a vast number of garments really be necessary or was the stylist taking advantage of a buyer with famously deep pockets? She wondered what event the French industrialist was taking her to that required the over-the-top evening gown. She was not required to model any other clothing for his inspection. That was a relief for, stripped of her usual image and denied her streetwise fashion, she felt strangely naked and vulnerable clad in items that did not belong to her.

Navarre was on the phone talking in English when she returned to his side. As they walked back through the store he continued the conversation, his deep drawl a low-pitched sexy purr, and she guessed that he was chatting to a woman. They returned to the hotel in silence. She wanted to go home and collect some of her own things but was trying to pick the right moment in which to make that request. Navarre vanished into the bedroom, reappearing in a light grey suit ten minutes later and walking past her.

'I'm going out. I'll see you tomorrow,' he told her silkily.

Her smooth brow furrowed. 'Do I have to stay here?'

'That's the deal,' he confirmed with a dismissive lack of interest that set her teeth on edge.

It was after midnight when Navarre came back to his suite with Jacques still at his heels. He had forgotten about Tawny so it was a surprise to walk in and see the lounge softly lit. Three heads turned from the table between them to glance at him, three of the individuals, members of his security team, instantly rising upright to greet him with an air of discomfiture beneath Jacques's censorious appraisal.

From the debris it was clear there had been takeout food eaten, and from the cards and small heaps of coins visible several games of poker. Tawny didn't stand up. She stayed where she was curled up barefoot on the sofa.

Navarre shifted a hand in dismissal of his guards. Tawny had yet to break into her new wardrobe, for she wore faded skinny jeans with slits over the knee and a tee with a skeleton motif. Her hair fell in a torrent of spiralling curls halfway down her back, much longer than he had appreciated and providing a frame for her youthful piquant face that gave her an almost fey quality.

'Where did you get those clothes from?' he asked bluntly.

'I gave Elise a list of things that I needed along with my keys and she was kind enough to go and pack a bag for me. I didn't think that what I wore behind closed doors would matter.' Tawny gazed back at him in silent challenge, striving not to react in any way to the fact that he was drop-dead gorgeous, particularly with that dark shadow of stubble roughening his masculine jawline and accentuating the sensual curve of his beautifully shaped mouth.

Navarre bent to lift the open sketch pad resting on the arm of the sofa. It was an amusing caricature of Elise and instantly recognisable as such. He flicked it back and found another, registering that she had drawn each of her companions. 'You did these? They're good.'

Tawny shifted a narrow shoulder in dismissal. 'Not good enough to pay the bills,' she said wryly, thinking of how often her mother had criticised her for choosing to study art rather than a subject that the older woman had deemed to be of more practical use.

'A talent nonetheless.'

'Where am I supposed to sleep tonight?' Tawny asked flatly, in no mood to debate the topic.

'You can sleep on the sofa,' Navarre told her without hesitation, irritated that he had not thought of her requirements soon enough to ask for a suite with an extra bedroom. 'It will only be for two nights and then we'll be leaving London.'

'To go where?'

'Further north.' With that guarded reply, he walked into the bedroom and a couple of minutes later he reappeared with a bedspread and a pillow in his arms. He deposited them on a chair nearby and then with a nod departed again. He moved with the fluid grace of a dancer and he emanated sex appeal like a force field, she acknowledged tautly, her eyes veiling as she struggled to suppress a tiny little twisting flicker of response to him.

'You know…a real gentleman would offer a lady the bed,' Tawny called in his wake.

Navarre shot her a sardonic glance, green eyes bright as jewels between the thick luxuriance of his black lashes as he drawled, 'I've never been a gentleman and I very much doubt that you're a lady in the original sense of the word.'

CHAPTER THREE

THE next morning, Navarre watched Tawny sleep, curls that melded from bright red to copper tipped with strawberry-blonde ends spilling out across the pale smooth skin of her narrow shoulders, dark lashes low over delicate cheekbones, her plump pink pouting mouth incredibly sexy. He brushed a colourful strand of hair away from her face. 'Wake up,' he urged.

Tawny woke with a start, eyes shooting wide as she half sat up. 'What?'

Navarre had retreated several feet to give her space. 'Time to rise. You have a busy day ahead of you.'

Tawny rubbed her eyes like a child and hugged her pyjama-clad knees before muttering, 'Doing what?'

'A beautician and a hairstylist will be here this afternoon to help you to prepare for this evening's event. A jeweller will be here in an hour. The bathroom's free,' he informed her coolly. 'What do you want for breakfast?'

'The full works—I'm always starving first thing,' she told him, scrambling off the sofa and folding the spread with efficient hands, a lithe figure clad in cotton pyjama pants and a camisole top. 'Where are you taking me this evening?'

'A movie awards ceremony.'

Her eyes widened. 'Wow…fancy, so that's what the boring grey dress is for—'

'It isn't boring—'

'Take it from me, it was boring enough that my mother would have admired it,' she declared unimpressed, heading off to the bathroom, pert buttocks swaying above long slim legs.

'Wear one of your new outfits,' he told her before she vanished from view.

'But if we're not going out until this evening—'

'You need a practice run. Get into role for the jeweller's benefit,' Navarre advised.

Tawny rummaged through the huge pile of garment bags, carriers and boxes that had been delivered to the suite the night before. She had hung the bags on the door of the wardrobe but had felt uneasy about the prospect of stowing away the clothing in a room that he was using. She set out a narrow check skirt and a silk top. It was a dull conventional outfit but, for what he had promised to pay her for her services as a fake fiancée, she was willing to make an effort. She took the undies into the bathroom and went for a shower, using his shower gel but keeping her hair out of the water because she did not want the hassle of drying it.

Navarre watched her walk back across the carpet to join him at the breakfast table, her heart-shaped face composed, her bright curls bouncing like tongues of flame across her silk-clad shoulders. His masculine gaze took in the pouting curve of her breasts, her tiny waist and the long tight line of the skirt, below which her shapely legs were very much in evidence. *'Tu es belle…y*ou are beautiful, *mignonne.'*

Tawny rolled her eyes, unconvinced, recognising the

sophisticated and highly experienced charm of a womaniser in his coolly measuring appraisal. 'I clean up well.'

Navarre liked her deprecating manner and admired the
more telling fact that she had walked right past a mirror
without even pausing to admire her own reflection. The
waiter arrived with a breakfast trolley. Although Tawny
knew him the young man studiously avoided looking at
her even while she was making her selections from the hot
food on offer. Her cheeks burned as she realised that the
staff would naturally have assumed that she was sleeping
with Navarre.

Navarre had never seen a woman put away that much
food at one sitting. Tawny ate daintily but she had a very
healthy appetite. After her second cup of coffee and final
slice of toast she pushed away her plate, relaxed back in
her chair and smiled. 'Now I can face the day.'

'Do you think you've eaten enough to keep you going
until lunchtime?' Navarre could not resist that teasing
comment.

Her eyes widened in suggestive dismay. 'Are you saying that I can't have a snack before then?'

The biter bit, Navarre laughed out loud, very much
amused. In that instant, eyes glittering with brilliance between dense black lashes that reminded her very much of
lace, he was so charismatic he just took her breath away
and left her staring at his handsome face. It was impossible to look away and as his gaze narrowed in intensity
her tummy flipped as if she had gone down in a lift too
fast.

Navarre thrust back his chair and sprang upright to extend a hand down to her. Breathless and bemused, Tawny
took his hand without thought and stood up as well. Long
fingers framed her cheekbone and he lowered his arrogant dark head to allow the tip of his tongue to barely

skim along the fullness of her lower lip. She opened her mouth instinctively, her entire body tingling with an electric awareness that raised every tiny hair on her skin. His tongue darted into the moist interior of her mouth in a light teasing flicker that skimmed the inner surface of her lip. It was so *incredibly* sexy it made her shiver as if she were standing in a force-ten gale. Desire rose in her in an uncontrollable wave, screaming through her, spreading heat and hunger into every erotic part of her body. Helplessly she leant forwards, longing to be closer to him, insanely conscious of the tight fullness of her breasts and the hot, damp sting of awareness pulsing between her thighs. With a masculine growl vibrating deep in his throat, he finally kissed her with sweet sensual force, giving her the exact level of strength and urgency that her entire being craved from him.

When in the midst of that passionate embrace Navarre suddenly stopped kissing her and angled his head back, Tawny was utterly bewildered.

'*C'est parfait!* You're really good at this.' Navarre gazed down at her with eyes as ice-cold as running water. 'Anyone seeing such a kiss would believe we were lovers. That pretence of intimacy is all that is required to make us convincing.'

Tawny turned white and then suddenly red as a tide of mortification gripped her but she contrived to veil her eyes and stand her ground. 'Thank you,' she replied as if she had known all along what he was doing and had responded accordingly.

She was mentally kicking herself hard for having responded to his advances as if she were his newest girlfriend. How could she have done that? How could she have lost all control and forgotten who he was and who she was and exactly why they were together? He was paying her, for goodness sake! There was nothing else between them, no intimate relationship of any kind, she reminded herself brutally. On his terms she was something between an employee and a paid escort and not at all the sort of woman he would normally spend time with. Yet she had found that kiss more exciting than any she had ever experienced and would probably have still been in his arms had he not chosen to end that embarrassing little experiment. He had given his fake fiancée a fake kiss and she had fallen for it as though it were real.

Why on earth did she find Navarre Cazier so attractive? He might be extraordinarily good-looking but surely it took more than cheap physical chemistry to break down her barriers? As a rule she was standoffish with men and a man had to work at engaging her interest. All Navarre had done was insult her, so how could she possibly be attracted to him? Infuriated by her weakness, she took a seat as far away from him as she could get.

A warning knock sounded on the door before it opened to show Jacques shepherding in two men, one carrying a large case. It was the jeweller, complete with his own bodyguard. Navarre brought her forwards to sit beside him. Stiff as a doll and wearing a fixed smile, she sat down and looked on in silence as the older man displayed a range of fabulous rings featuring different stones.

'What do you like?' Navarre prompted.

'Aren't diamonds supposed to be a girl's best friend?' Tawny quipped and the diamond tray immediately rose uppermost.

Navarre took her small hand in his. 'Choose the one you like best.'

His hand was so much larger than hers, darker, stronger, and all she could think about for an horrific few moments was how that hand would feel if it were to touch her body, stroking…*caressing.* What the heck was the matter with her brain? Hungry hormones and heated embarrassment mushrooming inside her, Tawny bent her head over the diamond display and pointed blindly. 'May I try that one?'

'A pink diamond…a superb choice,' the jeweller remarked, passing the ring to Navarre, who eased the ring onto Tawny's finger. It was a surprisingly good fit.

'I like it,' Navarre declared.

'It is just *unbelievably* gorgeous!' Tawny gushed, batting her lashes like fly swats in response to the squeeze hold he had on her wrist.

Navarre shot her a quelling look in punishment for that vocal eruption while the purchase was being made. Several shallow jewel cases were removed from the case and opened to display an array of matching diamond pieces. Without recourse to her, Navarre selected a pair of drop earrings, a slender bracelet and a brooch, which she gathered were being offered on loan for her to wear that evening.

'Try not to behave like an airhead,' Navarre advised when they were alone again. 'It irritates me.'

Tawny resisted the urge to admit even to herself that awakening his irritation was preferable to receiving no reaction from him at all, for that made her sound childish. Had he not been hovering, however, she would have reached for her sketch pad, for his unmistakeably French character traits amused her. Regardless of the apparent passion of that kiss, she was convinced that Navarre Cazier rarely lost control or focus. He was arrogant, cool, reserved and extremely sure of himself.

'My English lawyer will be calling in shortly with the confidentiality agreement which you have to sign,' Navarre informed her, shrugging back a pristine shirt cuff to check the time. 'I have business to take care of this afternoon. I will see you later.'

'Can I go out? I'm going stir crazy in here,' she confided.

'If you go out or contact anyone our agreement will be null and void,' Navarre spelt out coldly. 'Elise will be keeping you company while I'm out.'

Elise arrived and he had barely left the room before Tawny's sketch pad was in her hand and she was drawing. Capturing Navarre on paper with strong dark lines, she drew him as she had seen him while she modelled evening gowns for him at the department store the day before. *'Sensationnel,'* he had purred with his charismatic smile, but she had known meeting his detached gaze that the compliment was essentially meaningless for she meant nothing to him beyond being a means to an end. In the cartoon she depicted the stylist as a curvaceous man killer, standing behind her and the true focus of his masculine admiration. It was artistic licence but it expressed Tawny's growing distrust of Navarre Cazier's astute intelligence, for she would have given much to understand why he felt the need to *hire* a woman to pretend to be his fiancée. What was he hiding from her or from the rest of the world? What were the secrets that he was so determined to keep from public view on that laptop? Secrets of such importance that he was willing to hold Tawny incommunicado and a virtual prisoner within his hotel suite to ensure that she could not share them…

'May I see what you have drawn?' Elise asked.

Tawny grimaced.

'If it's the boss I won't tell anyone,' she promised, and Tawny extended her pad.

Elise laughed. 'You have caught him well but he is not a lech.'

'A cartoon is a joke, Elise, not a character reference,' Tawny explained. 'You're very loyal to him.'

'I was in lust with him for the first year I worked for him.' Elise wrinkled her nose in an expression of chagrin. 'It hurts my pride to remember how I was. He seemed so beautiful I couldn't take my eyes off him.'

'And then he *speaks*,' Tawny slotted in flatly.

'No, no!' Elise laughed at that crack. 'No, I realised what a fool I was being once I saw him with his ladies. Only the most beautiful catch his eye and even they cannot hold him longer than a few weeks, particularly if they demand too much of his time and attention. He would never get involved with an employee, but he is very much a single guy, who wants to keep it that way.'

'I can't fault him for that. Who is the current lady in his life?'

Elise winced and suddenly scrambled upright again as if she had just remembered who Tawny was and what she was supposed to be doing with her. 'I'm sorry, I can't tell you. That is confidential information.'

Tawny went pink. 'No problem. I understand.'

A suave well-dressed lawyer arrived with the confidentiality agreement soon afterwards. He explained the basics of the document and gave it to her to read. When she had finished reading what seemed to be a fairly standard contract she borrowed his pen to sign it and, satisfied, he departed. Elise ordered a room-service lunch for them and when it was delivered Tawny noticed the waiter flicking his eyes repeatedly to the napkin on her lap. She ran her fingers through the folds and felt the stiffness of paper. As she withdrew what she assumed to be a note she pushed it into the pocket of her jeans for reading when she was alone and then shook out the napkin, her heart thumping. A note? But from whom? And about what? Julie was the only member of staff she had got close to and why would Julie be trying to communicate with her again?

As if to apologise for her caginess about her employer's private life, Elise told Tawny about her boyfriend, Michel, who was a chef in Paris and how difficult the couple found it to see each other with Michel usually working nights when Elise was most often free. After a light meal, Tawny went off to the bathroom to unfurl the note and felt terribly guilty about doing so, knowing that her companion was supposed to be ensuring that no such communications were taking place. Unfortunately for Navarre, Elise just wasn't observant enough to be an effective guard.

'If you call…' the note ran and a London phone number followed. 'Information about Navarre Cazier is worth a lot of money.'

It was typed and unsigned. Tawny thrust the note back into her pocket with a frown of discomfiture. Was this a direct approach from the journalist who had tried to bribe Julie into doing his dirty work for him by stealing Navarre's laptop? If it was the same journalist he was certainly persistent in his underhand methods. Was he hoping that Tawny would make use of her current seemingly privileged position to spy for him and gather information about Navarre Cazier?

Distaste filled her. She felt slightly soiled at having even read the note. Navarre Cazier might think she had no standards because she had agreed to let him pay her to act as his fiancée, but Tawny had only agreed to that role because she was determined to ensure her grandmother Celestine's continuing security in her retirement home. If it had only been a matter of personal enrichment, if Navarre had not had the power to force Tawny to give up her employment, she would have refused his offer outright, she reflected unhappily. She would never forget the lesson of how her own mother's financial greed had badly hurt Celestine. Even family affection had proved insufficient to avert that tragedy and Tawny did not think she would ever find it possible to fully forgive her mother for what she had done to the old lady.

When she returned to the lounge Elise was taking delivery of a substantial set of designer luggage. 'For your new clothes,' she explained. 'You'll be travelling tomorrow.'

Feeling uncomfortable with the other woman after secretly reading that forbidden note, Tawny used the delivery as an excuse to return to the bedroom and pack the contents of all the bags, boxes and garment carriers into the cases instead. By the time she had finished doing that the beautician and her assistant had arrived with a case of tools and cosmetics and Tawny had to wrap herself in a towel to let them start work. What followed was a whirlwind of activity in the bedroom, which was taken over, and the afternoon wore on while she was waxed and plucked and massaged and moisturised and painted. By the time it was over she was convinced that there was not an inch of her body that had not been treated and enhanced in some way. As a woman who devoted very little time to her looks she found it something of a revelation to appreciate how much stuff she could have been doing to add polish to her appearance.

By the time the hairdresser arrived, Tawny was climbing the walls with boredom, a mood that was not helped by the stylist's visible dismay when confronted by Tawny's tempestuous mane of spiralling ringlets. When her hair was done, she was made up, and only when that was over could she finally don the grey lace evening gown. She was looking at herself in the mirror and grimacing at how old-fashioned she thought she looked when Elise brought in the diamond jewellery and Tawny put on the ring, the drop earrings and the bracelet. Studying the brooch, she suddenly had an idea and she bent down and pulled up the skirt to hold it above the knee, where it cascaded down in ruffles to her ankles. Ignoring Elise's dropped jaw, she anchored the skirt there with the brooch, straightened, pushed up the long tight sleeves of her dress to her elbow and bared her shoulders as well. The dress, magically, acquired a totally different vibe.

Navarre, waiting impatiently in the lounge to shower and change, glanced up as the bedroom door swung open and there she was, framed in the doorway. The classic elegant image he had expected was nowhere to be seen. There she stood, her magnificent hair tumbling in a rather wild torrent round her shoulders, her face glowing with subtle make-up, dominated by eyes bright as stars and a soft ripe mouth tinted the colour of raspberries. She looked so beautiful that he was stunned. That the dress he had chosen had been mysteriously transformed into sexy saloon girl-style went right past him because he was much too busy appreciating her satin smooth white shoulders and the slender, shapely perfection of her knees and ankles.

The silence filled the room and stretched as Tawny studied him expectantly.

'Is the shower free?' Navarre enquired smoothly, compressing his stubborn mouth on any comment relating to her appearance. She was working for him. He was paying for the entire display. Any remark, after all, would be both superfluous and inappropriate.

CHAPTER FOUR

TAWNY knew she had never looked so good and while she waited for Navarre to get ready she tried not to feel offended by his silence on that score. What was the matter with her? He was not a date, he was not required to pay her compliments and at least he hadn't complained about the liberties she had taken with the grey lace shroud he had picked for her to wear. Shouldn't she be grateful that he was maintaining a polite distance? Did she want the boundary lines between them to blur again? She certainly didn't want another kiss that made her feel as if she were burning up like a flame inside her own skin. Well, actually she *did* want one but that was not a prompting powered by her brain, it was more of a deeply mortifying craving. She told herself that there was no way that she would be stupid enough to succumb to his magnetic sexual allure a second time. Forewarned was forearmed.

'Let's go,' Navarre urged, joining her in an exquisitely tailored dinner jacket, the smooth planes of his freshly shaven features as beautiful as a dark angel's.

In the lift she found it a challenge to drag her eyes from the flawless perfection of his visage. 'Don't you think you should finally tell me where we're going?' she pressed.

'The Golden Awards and the showbiz party afterwards,' he revealed.

Her eyes widened in shock. She struggled to be cool and not reveal the fact that she was impressed to death. A huge number of well-known international celebrities would be attending the opulent Golden Movie Awards ceremony. The GMAs were a famous annual event, beloved of the glitterati. 'All the press will be there,' she said weakly, suddenly grasping why she was wearing a very expensive designer dress and a striking array of diamonds.

Acutely aware of the abnormal number of staff at Reception waiting to watch their departure, Tawny had to struggle to keep her head held high, but there was nothing that she could do to stop her face burning. Everybody would think she was sleeping with him; of course they would think that! People always went for the sleaziest explanation of the seemingly incomprehensible and why else would a chambermaid be dolled up in a designer frock and walking with a billionaire? Navarre escorted her out to the limousine.

'You've got some nerve taking someone like me with you to the Golden Awards,' Tawny dared to comment as the luxury car pulled away from the kerb.

Navarre studied her with amusement gleaming in his eyes. '*Mais non.* No man who looks at you will wonder why I am with you.'

'You mean they'll all think that I have to be absolutely amazing in bed!' Tawny retorted unimpressed.

Navarre shifted a broad shoulder in a tiny shrug that was very Gallic, understated and somehow deeply cool. 'I have no objection to inspiring envy.'

Tawny swallowed the angry words brimming on her tongue and breathed in slow and deep, while staunchly reminding herself of Celestine's need for her financial assistance.

'You're wearing an engagement ring,' Navarre reminded her drily. 'That puts you into a very different category, *ma petite*.'

'Don't call me that— I'm not *that* small!' Tawny censured.

A grin as unexpected as it was charismatic momentarily slashed his wide sensual mouth. 'You are considerably smaller than I am and very slim—'

'Skinny,' Tawny traded argumentatively. 'Don't dress it up. I eat like a horse but I've always been skinny.'

'We met at an art gallery…our fake first meeting,' Navarre extended when she frowned at him in bewilderment. 'If you are asked you will say that we met at an art showing here in London.'

'If I must.'

'You must. I refuse to say that I met the woman I intend to marry while she was changing my bed,' Navarre told her unapologetically.

'Snob,' Tawny told him roundly, crossing her legs and suddenly aware of the sweep of his gaze finally resting on the long length of thigh she had unintentionally exposed as the skirt of her gown slid back from her legs. As she lifted her head and encountered those spectacular eyes of his there was a knot of tension at the tender heart of her where she was unaccustomed to feeling anything.

Hard as a rock as he scrutinised that silken expanse of thigh, Navarre was exasperated enough by his body's indiscipline and her false impression of him to give a sardonic laugh of disagreement. 'I am not a snob. I worked in hotel kitchens to pay my way as a schoolboy. Survival was never a walk in the park when I was growing up and I have never forgotten how hard I had to work for low pay.'

Filled with all the embarrassment of someone labelled a thief and the new knowledge that he did have experience of working long hours for a small wage, Tawny evaded his gaze and smoothed down her skirt. She thought of the very generous tips he had left for her on his previous stays at the hotel and shame washed over her in a choking wave of regret. She wished she had never met Julie and never listened to her clever lies, for she had betrayed Navarre's trust. His generosity should have been rewarded by the attention of honest, dependable staff.

The car was slowing down in the heavy flow of traffic, gliding past crowded pavements to come to a halt outside the brightly lit theatre where the Goldens were to be held. As Tawny glimpsed the crush of sightseers behind the crash barriers, the stand of journalists, a presenter standing talking beside men with television cameras and the red carpet stretching to the entrance, something akin to panic closed her throat over.

'Don't stop to answer questions. Let me do the talking if there are any. Just smile,' Navarre instructed.

Tawny found it a challenge to breathe as she climbed out of the car. As cameras flashed she saw spots in front of her eyes and Navarre's steadying hand at her elbow was appreciated. He exchanged a light word with the attractive presenter who appeared to know him and steered her on smoothly into the building. An usher showed them to their seats inside the theatre. No sooner had they sat down than people began to stop in the aisle to greet Navarre and he made a point of introducing her as his fiancée. Time after time she saw surprise blossom in faces that Navarre should apparently be on the brink of settling down with one woman. That sceptical reaction told her all she needed to know about his reputation as a womaniser, she reflected sourly. Furthermore it seemed to her as though it might take more than diamonds and a designer gown to persuade his friends that she was the genuine article.

She watched as renowned actors and directors walked

up to the stage to collect awards and give speeches. Her hands ached from clapping and her mouth from smiling. It was a strain to feel so much on show and something of a relief when he indicated that it was time to leave.

As they crossed the foyer on their way out of the theatre a musical female voice called breathily, 'Navarre!' and he came to a dead halt.

Tia Castelli, exquisite as a china doll in a stunning blue chiffon dress teamed with a fabulous sapphire pendant, was hurrying down the staircase that led up to the private theatre boxes. Tawny couldn't take her eyes off the beauty, who was very much the screen goddess of her day. Earlier she had watched Tia collect a trophy for her outstanding performance in her most recent film in which she had played a woman being terrorised by a former boyfriend, and she had marvelled that she could be even seated that close to a living legend.

'And you must be Tawny!' Tia exclaimed, bending down with a brilliant smile to kiss Tawny lightly on both cheeks while cameras went crazy all around them as every newshound in their vicinity rushed to capture photos of the celebrated actress. Tawny was knocked sideways by that unexpectedly friendly greeting. Tia was extraordinarily beautiful in the flesh and, confronted by such a very famous figure, Tawny felt tongue-tied.

'Congratulations—I was so happy to hear your news and Navarre's,' Tia continued. 'Join Luke and I in our limo. We're heading to the same party.'

'How on earth did you get so friendly with Tia Castelli?' Tawny hissed as security guards escorted them back out via the red carpet.

'My first boss in private banking took care of her investments. I've known her a long time,' Navarre responded calmly.

Tia paused to greet fans and pose for the TV cameras while her tall, skinny, unshaven husband, clad in tight jeans, a crumpled blue velvet jacket and a black trilby as befitted the image of a hard-living rock star, ignored every attempt to slow down his progress and headed straight for the waiting limousine. With a rueful sigh, Navarre urged Tawny in the same direction and wished, not for the first time, that Tia were less impulsive and more cautious.

'So you're going to marry Navarre,' Luke Convery commented, his Irish accent unexpectedly melodic and soft as he introduced himself carelessly and studied Tawny with assessing brown eyes. 'What have you got that the rest of them haven't?'

'*This...*' Tawny showed off the opulent pink diamond while finding it impossible not to wonder just how much younger Luke was than his wife. They didn't even look like a couple, for in comparison to her polished Hollywood glamour he dressed like a tramp. She doubted that the musician was out of his twenties while Tia had to be well into her thirties, for her incredibly successful career had spanned Tawny's lifetime. She thought it was good that just for once it was an older woman with a younger man rather than the other way round, and she was warmed by the way Luke immediately reached for his wife's hand when she got into the car and the couple exchanged a mutually affectionate smile.

By all accounts, Tia Castelli deserved a little happiness, for she had led an impossibly eventful life from the moment she was spotted by a film director as a naive schoolgirl in a Florentine street and starred in her first blockbuster movie as the child of a broken marriage. She was a mesmerising actress, whom the camera truly loved. Admittedly Tia was no stranger to emotion or tragedy, for violent and unfaithful husbands, jealous lovers and nervous breakdowns with all the attendant publicity had all featured at one point or another in the star's life. She had suffered divorce, widowhood and a miscarriage during her only pregnancy.

'Let me see the ring,' Tia urged, stretching out a be-jewelled hand weighted with diamonds. 'Oh, I *love* it.'

'You haven't got a finger free for another diamond,' Luke told his wife drily. 'How long do we have to stay at this party?'

'A couple of hours?' Tia gave him a pleading look of appeal.

'It'll be really boring,' Luke forecast moodily, his lower lip coming out in a petulant pout.

Beside her Navarre stiffened and Tia looked as though she might be about to burst into tears. Navarre asked Tia's husband about his upcoming European tour with his rock group, the moment of tension ebbed and shortly afterwards they arrived at the glitzy hotel where the party was being held. Tia was mobbed by paparazzi outside the hotel and lingered to give an impromptu interview to a TV pre-senter. Tawny was startled when Navarre stepped slightly behind her to pose for a photo, mentioning her name and their supposed engagement with the relaxed assurance of a man who might have known her for years rather than mere days. It occurred to her that he was quite an actor in his own right, able to conceal his essential indifference to her behind a convincing façade as though she were in-deed precious to him. While he spoke the warmth of his tall, strong physique burned down her slender spine like a taunting lick of flame and the faint scent of some ex-pensive cologne underscored by clean, husky masculin-ity filled her nostrils and suddenly her body was going haywire with awareness, breasts swelling, legs trembling as she remembered that earth-shattering kiss.

One freakin' kiss, Tawny thought with furious resentment, and she had fallen apart at the seams. He hadn't even made a pass at her. She had to be fair, he wasn't the pawing type, indeed he never laid a finger on her without good reason, but even so, when he got close, every skin cell in her body leapt and dived as if she were a dizzy teenager in the grip of her first crush.

'Are you always this tense?' Navarre enquired.

'Only around you,' she told him, knowing that there was more than one way to read that reply.

Trailing adoring hangers-on like a vibrant kite followed by fluttering ribbons, Tia surged up to them as soon as they entered the function room and complained that Luke had already taken off and abandoned her.

'He hates these things,' she complained ruefully as Navarre immediately took on the task of ushering her to her prominently placed table.

Tia was very much what Tawny would have expected of a beautiful international star. She had to have constant attention and wasn't too fussy about how she went about getting it. She was very familiar with Navarre, touching his arm continually as she talked, smiling sexily up at him, employing every weapon in the considerable armoury of her beauty to keep him by her side and hold his interest. A proper fiancée, Tawny reflected wryly, would have wanted to shoot Tia and bury her deep.

'You should tell him you don't like it,' Luke whispered mockingly in Tawny's ear, making her jump because she had not realised he had come to stand beside her.

'I've got no complaints. Your wife is the life and soul of the party,' Tawny answered lightly, as if she were quite unconcerned when in fact she had felt invisible in Tia's radius.

'No, she likes handsome men around her,' Luke Convery

contradicted, watching the Italian blonde hold court at her table surrounded by attentive males, his demeanour a resentful combination of admiration and annoyance. As if he was determined to defy that view he draped an arm round Tawny's taut shoulders and she stiffened in surprise.

Across the room, Navarre's glittering green gaze narrowed to rest on Tawny, watching her lift her face to look up into Luke Convery's eyes and suddenly laugh. They looked remarkably intimate, he noted in surprise. How had that happened between virtual strangers? Or was the luscious redhead a quick study when it came to impressing rich and famous men? Anger broke like a river bursting its banks through Navarre's usual rock-solid self-discipline and he vaulted upright to take immediate action.

'You should try staying by Tia's side,' Tawny was saying warily to Luke Convery.

'Been there, done that. It doesn't work but you might have more luck with that angle.' The musician shot her a challenging appraisal from brooding dark eyes. 'If you're engaged to the guy, why are you letting Tia take over?'

Reminded of her role, Tawny flushed and headed off to the cloakroom to escape the awkward exchange. How was she supposed to react when a household name with a face that could have given Helen of Troy a run for her money was flirting like mad with her supposed fiancé? When she returned to the party, she was taken aback to see Navarre poised near the doors, evidently awaiting her reappearance. When he saw her, he immediately frowned and jerked his arrogant head to urge her over to him.

'What have you been doing? Where have you been?' he demanded curtly.

Resenting his attitude, Tawny rolled her eyes. 'I was in the cloakroom, trying to discreetly avoid coming between you and the object of your affections.'

He followed her meaningful sidewise glance in the direction of Tia Castelli's table and his strong jawline clenched as though Tawny had insulted him. His eyes narrowed to rake over her with scorn. '*Drôle d'excuse…* what an excuse! Tia and I are old friends, nothing more. But I saw you giggling with Convery—'

'What do you mean by you "*saw*" me with Luke?' Tawny pressed hotly, hostile to both his intonation and his attitude. 'And I'm not the giggly type.'

Navarre flattened his wide sensual mouth into a forbidding line. 'We are supposed to be newly engaged. You are not here to amuse yourself. *Stay by my side.*'

'As long as you appreciate that I'm only doing it for the money,' Tawny shot back at him in an angry hiss, her face stiff with chagrin at his criticism of her behaviour.

'I'm unlikely to forget the fact that I'm paying for the pleasure of your company,' he retorted crushingly. 'That's a first for me!'

'You do surprise me.' Hot pink adorning her cheeks at that cutting retaliation, Tawny stuck to him like glue for the rest of the party. He circulated, one arm attached to Tawny as he made a point of introducing her as his future wife.

Tawny played up to the label, clinging to his arm, smiling up at him, laughing slavishly at the mildest joke or story and generally behaving as if he were the centre of her world. And for what he was paying for the show, she told herself ruefully, he deserved to be.

'Did you have to behave like a bimbo?' Navarre growled as she climbed back into the limousine at the end of the evening, shoulders drooping as exhaustion threatened to claim her.

'In this scenario it works. As you said yourself, if we seem unsuited, nobody will be surprised when the engagement only lasts for five minutes,' Tawny retorted, thoroughly irritated at receiving yet more vilification from his corner. Could she do nothing right in his eyes? What exactly did he want from her? 'Personally, I think I put in a pretty good performance.'

A silence that implied he had been less than impressed stretched between them all the way back to the hotel. In the lift he stabbed the button for a lower floor. 'Elise has offered to share her room with you tonight so that you don't have to use the sofa again,' he informed her glacially. 'I believe she already has had your belongings moved for your convenience.'

Relief filled Tawny as she stepped out of the lift and found the tall blonde bodyguard waiting to greet her. With Elise, she could take off her fancy glad rags, climb into her pjs and relax, which was exactly what she was most longing to do at that instant.

Navarre absorbed the alacrity of Tawny's departure from the lift, frowning at the strangely appealing sound of the giggling she had said she didn't do trilling down the corridor just before the lift doors closed again. He had never had a woman walk away from him before without a word or a glance and his eyes momentarily flashed as though someone had lit a fire behind them. He could not accuse Tawny Baxter of attempting to ensnare him, but he recalled the manner in which she had melted into that kiss and smiled, ego soothed. It was not a very nice smile.

CHAPTER FIVE

'Oh...my...goodness!' Tawny squealed in Navarre's ear as she squashed her face up against the window of the helicopter to get a better view of the medieval fortress they were flying over, a sixteenth-century tower house complete with a Victorian gothic extension. It was late afternoon. 'It's a castle, a *real* castle! Are we really going to be staying there?'

'*Oui,*' Navarre confirmed drily.

'You are *so* spoilt!' Tawny exclaimed loudly, winning Jacques's startled scrutiny from the front seat as she turned briefly to shoot his employer a reproachful look. 'You're going to be staying in a genuine castle and you're not even excited! Not even a little bit excited?'

'You're excited enough for both of us,' Navarre countered. His attention was commanded against his will by the vibrant glow of her heart-shaped face and the anticipation writ large there, eyes starry, lush peachy mouth showing a glimpse of small white teeth. Adults rarely demonstrated that much enthusiasm for anything and, to a man who kept all emotion under strict lock and key, there was something ridiculously appealing about her complete lack of inhibition.

The helicopter, which had carried them north from their private flight to Edinburgh and lunch at a smart hotel there, landed in a paddock within full view of the castle. Navarre sprang out in advance of Tawny and then swung round to lift her out. 'I could've managed!' she told him pointedly, smoothing down her clothing as though he had rumpled her.

'Not without a step in that skirt,' Navarre traded with all the superiority of a male accustomed to disembarking from such craft with a woman in tow.

Tawny had slept like a log the night before in the room she had shared with Elise. Similar in age, the two young women had chattered over a late supper, exchanging innocuous facts about friends and families.

'The boss warned me that I had to be sure to feed you!' Elise had teased, watching, impressed, as Tawny demolished a plate of sandwiches.

Now she was in the Scottish Highlands for the weekend but Navarre had only divulged their destination after he had invited her to join him for breakfast in his suite that morning, when he had also filled her in on a few useful facts about their hosts.

Tawny was rather nervous at the prospect of meeting Sam and Catrina Coulter. Sam was the extremely wealthy owner of the Coulter Centax Corporation. Catrina, whom Navarre had admitted was an ex, was Sam's second, much younger wife and formerly a very successful English model. The couple had no children but Sam had had a son by his first marriage, who had died prematurely in an accident.

'So is this where Sam and Catrina live all the year round?' Tawny asked curiously as they walked towards the Range Rover awaiting them. 'It must be pretty desolate in winter.'

'They don't own Strathmore Castle, they're renting it

for the season,' Navarre told her wryly. 'Sam's very into shooting and fishing.'

Sam Coulter was in his sixties, a trim bespectacled man with grey hair and a keen gaze. Catrina, a beautiful brunette with big brown eyes and an aggressively bright smile, towered over her empire building husband, who made up for what he lacked in height with his large personality. Refreshments were served before the fire in the atmospheric Great Hall that had walls studded with a display of medieval weaponry, fabulous early oak furniture and a tartan carpet. Catrina made a big thing out of cooing over Tawny's engagement ring and tucked a friendly hand into the younger woman's arm to lead her upstairs, but there was neither true warmth nor sincerity in her manner. Only when Catrina left Navarre and Tawny in the same room did it occur to Tawny that they were expected to occupy the same bed.

'We're supposed to share?' she whispered within seconds of the door closing behind their hostess.

'What else would you expect?'

Unfortunately Tawny had not thought about the possibility. Now she scanned the room. There was no sofa, nothing other than the four-poster bed for the two of them to sleep on, and something akin to panic gripped her. 'You could say you snore and keep me awake *and*—'

'You're not that naive. We must share the bed. It is only for two nights,' Navarre drawled.

'I'm shy about sharing beds,' Tawny warned him.

Navarre studied her, intently. 'I'm *not*,' he told her without hesitation, flashing her a wickedly amused smile.

A painful flush lit Tawny's complexion. But the mesmerising charm of his smile at that instant knocked her sideways and her susceptible heart went boom-boom-

boom inside her ribcage. 'I really don't want to share a room with you.'

'You must have expected this set-up,' Navarre said very drily. 'Engaged couples rarely sleep in separate beds these days.'

It was a fair point and Tawny winced in acknowledgement. 'I didn't think about it.'

'We're stuck with the arrangement,' Navarre countered in a tone of finality. 'Or is this a ploy aimed at demanding more money from me? Is that what lies behind these antiquated protests?'

Tawny froze in astonishment, affronted by the suggestion. 'No, it darned well is not! How dare you suggest that? I just haven't shared a bed with a guy before—'

Navarre quirked a sardonic black brow. 'What? *Never?* I don't believe you.'

'Well, I don't care what you believe. You may sleep around but I never have!' Tawny slung back at him in furious self-defence.

'I didn't accuse you of sleeping around,' Navarre pointed out, his innate reserve and censure never more evident than in his hard gaze and the tough stubborn set of his strong jawline. 'Nor will I accept you throwing such impertinent remarks at me.'

'Point taken but I've always believed in calling a spade a spade and exclusive you're not!' Tawny responded, her temper still raw from the idea that he could think she was using the need to share a bed as an excuse to demand more money from him.

'Tonight we're sharing that bed, *ma petite*.' Navarre dealt her an intimidating appraisal, inviting her disagreement.

Tawny opened the case sited on the trunk at the foot of the bed to extract the outfit she had decided to wear for dinner. She loathed his conviction that she was unscrupulous and mercenary but she saw no point in getting into an argument with him. Navarre would probably fight tooth and claw to the death just to come out the winner. A row might be overheard and he would have reason to complain if anything happened to mar their pretence of being a happy couple.

'And by the way, I am exclusive with a woman for the duration of our time together.'

Bending over the case, Tawny reckoned that that would impose no great sacrifice on a man famous for never staying long with one woman and she murmured flatly, 'None of my business.'

Navarre breathed in slow and deep while on another level he drank in the intoxicating glimpses of slim, shapely thigh visible through the split in the back of her skirt. She straightened to shed her cardigan. Hunger uncoiled inside him. Every time she awakened his libido the effects got stronger, he acknowledged grimly, noting the way her bright rippling curls snaked down her slender spine, somehow drawing his attention to the fact that the top she wore was gossamer thin and revealed the pale delicate bra that encased her dainty breasts. *Merde alors,* he was behaving like a schoolboy salivating for his first glimpse of naked female flesh!

The chosen outfit draped over her arm, Tawny moved towards the wardrobe to hang the garment and as she did so she collided with Navarre's intent gaze. It was as if all the oxygen in her lungs were sucked out at once. Her heart went *thud* and she stilled in surprise as she recognised the sexual heat of that brutally masculine appraisal. 'Don't look at me like that,' she told him gruffly.

Navarre reached for her. 'I can't help it,' he purred.

'Yes, you can,' she countered shakily, longing with

every fibre of her rebellious being to be drawn closer to him while her brain screamed at her to slap him down and go into retreat. But there was something incredibly flattering about such a look of desire on a handsome man's face. Navarre had the ability to make her feel impossibly feminine and seductive, two qualities that she had never thought she possessed.

One hand resting on her hip, Navarre skimmed the knuckles of the other gently down the side of her face. 'You're beautiful, *ma petite*.'

Tawny had never seen herself as beautiful before and that single word had a hypnotic effect on her so that she looked up at him with shining ice-blue eyes. Teased for having red hair at school, she had grown into a sporty tomboy who lacked the curves required to attract the opposite sex. Boys had become her mates rather than her boyfriends, many of them using her as a step closer to her then best friend, a curvy little blonde. Curvy and blonde had become Tawny's yardstick of beauty and what Navarre Cazier could see in her was invisible to her own eyes.

Indecent warmth shimmied through Tawny from the caressing touch of his fingers and she wanted to lean into his hand, get closer on every level while that tightening sensation low in her body filled her with a sharp, deep craving. Struggling to control that dangerous sense of weakness, Tawny froze, torn between stepping closer and stepping back. While she was in the midst of that mental fight, Navarre bent his arrogant dark head and kissed her.

And it wasn't like that first teasing, tender kiss in London, it was a kiss full of an unashamed passion that shot through her bloodstream like an adrenalin rush. One kiss was nowhere near enough either. As his hungry, demanding mouth moved urgently on hers her fingers delved into his luxuriant black hair to hold him to her and she felt light-headed. His tongue delved and unleashed such acute hunger inside her that she gasped and instinctively pushed her taut, aching breasts into the inflexible wall of his broad chest. Gathering her closer, his hand splayed across her hips and she was instantly aware of the hard thrust of his erection. Her knees went weak as a dark tingling heat spread through her lower body in urgent response to his arousal.

He lifted her up and brought her down on the bed, still exchanging kiss for feverish kiss and suddenly she was on fire with longing, knowing exactly what she wanted and shocked by it. She wanted his weight on top of her to sate the ache at the core of her. She wanted to open her legs to cradle him but, ridiculously, her skirt was too tight.

In a sudden movement driven by that last idiotic thought, Tawny tore her lips from his. 'No, I don't want this!' she gasped, planting her hands on his wide shoulders to impose space between them.

Navarre immediately lifted back, face rigid with self-discipline. He vaulted back off the bed to stare down at her with scorching green eyes. 'Yes, you do want me as much as I want you. Together we're like a fire raging out of control and I don't know why you're imposing limits, unless it's because—'

'No, don't say it!' Tawny cut in, sitting up in a hurry and raking her tumbled hair off her brow with an impatient hand. 'Don't you dare say it!'

Navarre frowned in bewilderment. 'Say what?'

'Offer me more money to sleep with you…*don't you dare!*' she launched at him warningly.

Navarre elevated a sardonic black brow and stood straight and tall to gaze broodingly down at her. *'Mais c'est insensé*…that's crazy. I have not the slightest intention of offering you money for sex. I don't pay for it, never have, never will. Perhaps you're angling for me to make you that kind of an offer before you deliver between the sheets. But I'm afraid you've picked the wrong guy to work that ploy on.'

As that derisive little speech sank in Tawny went white with rage and sprang off the bed, the wild flare of her hot temper giving her a strong urge to slap him. But Navarre snapped hands like bands of steel round her wrists to hold her arms still by her side and prevent any other contact. '*No*,' he said succinctly. 'I won't tolerate that from any woman.'

High spots of colour bloomed in Tawny's cheeks as she jerked back from him, his icy intervention having doused her anger like a bucket of cold water. It didn't prevent her from still wanting to kill him though. 'I wasn't trying to put the idea in your head…OK? It's just I know what guys like you are like—'

'Like you know so many guys like me,' Navarre fielded witheringly.

'You're used to getting exactly what you want when you want and not taking no for an answer.'

'Not my problem,' Navarre countered glacially.

Tawny got changed in the bathroom. Her mouth was still swollen from his kisses, her body still all of a shiver and on edge from the sexual charge he put out. She mouthed a rude word at herself in the mirror, furious that she had lost control in his arms. She had genuinely feared that he might offer her money to include sex in their masquerade and she had tried to avert the risk of him uttering those fatal humiliating words, which would have reduced her to the level of a call girl. Unfortunately for her Navarre had actually suspected that she was sneakily making it clear to him that the offer of more money might make her amenable to sex.

Rage at that recollection threatening to engulf her in a rising red mist, Tawny anchored her towel tighter round her slim body and wrenched open the bathroom door in a sudden movement. 'I'm a virgin!' she launched across the room at him in stark condemnation. 'How many virgins do you know who sell themselves for money?'

I am not having this crazy argument, Navarre's clever brain told him soothingly as he cast down the remote control he had used to switch on the business news. She's a lunatic. I've hired a thief and a lunatic…

'I don't know any virgins,' Navarre told her truthfully. 'But that's probably because most of them keep quiet about their inexperience.'

'I don't see why I should keep quiet!' Tawny snapped, tilting her chin in challenge. 'You seem to be convinced that I would do anything for money…but I'm not like that.'

'We're not having this conversation,' Navarre informed her resolutely, stonily centring his attention back on the television screen.

But a flickering image of her entrancing slender profile in a towel with damp ringlets rioting round her small face still stayed inside his head. He didn't pay for sex. That was true. But there had definitely been a moment on that bed when, if he was equally honest, he would have given her just about anything to stay there warm and willing to fulfil his every fantasy. The ache of frustrated desire was with him still. Taking the moral high ground had never felt less satisfying. Even so his naturally suspicious mind kept on ticking. Why was she telling him that she was a virgin? Hadn't he read about some woman selling her virginity on the Internet to the highest bidder? Could Tawny believe that virgins had more sex appeal and value to the average male? Surely she didn't think that he would actually believe that a woman of twenty-three years of age was a total innocent? Did he look that naive and trusting?

Clad in a modestly styled green cocktail dress and impossibly high heels, Tawny descended the stairs by Navarre's side. They pretty much weren't speaking, which felt weird when he insisted on holding her hand. She was looking eagerly around her when Sam came to greet them, ushering them to the fire and the drinks waiting in the Great Hall. Having answered her questions about the old property, he offered them a tour.

The tower house was not as large as it had looked from the air and many of the rooms were rather pokey or awkwardly shaped. But Tawny adored the atmosphere created by the ancient stone walls and fireplaces and she looked at Catrina in surprise when she complained about the difficulty of heating the rooms and the remote location while her husband talked with single-minded enthusiasm about the outdoor pursuits available on the estate. The Victorian extension to the rear of the castle had been recently restored and contained a fabulous ballroom used for parties, modern utilities and staff quarters.

'You haven't been with Navarre long, have you?' Catrina remarked while the men were talking business over by the tall windows. The sun was going down for the day over the views of rolling heathland banded by distant mountains that had a purple hue in the fast-fading light.

Tawny smiled. 'I suppose it shows.'

Catrina sat down beside her. 'It does rather. He's obsessed with his work.'

'Successful men tend to be,' Tawny answered lightly, recalling that her half-sisters often complained about how preoccupied their husbands were with their business interests.

'Navarre will always be more excited about his latest deal than about you,' Catrina opined cattily.

'Oh, I don't think so.' Quite deliberately, Tawny flexed the fingers of the hand that bore the opulent diamond ring and glanced across the room at Navarre, admiring that bold bronzed masculine profile silhouetted against the window. As she turned back to Catrina she caught the other woman treating Navarre to a voracious look of longing. Navarre, she registered belatedly, had lit a fire in the other woman that even her marriage had yet to put out.

'Navarre won't change,' the beautiful brunette forecast thinly. 'He gets bored very easily. No woman ever lasts more than a few weeks in his bed.'

Tawny dealt her companion a calm appraisal. 'I don't begrudge Navarre his years of freedom. Most men eventually settle down with one woman just as he has,' she murmured sweetly. 'What we have together is special.'

'In what way?' Catrina enquired baldly and then she laughed and raised her voice, 'Navarre…what do you find most special about Tawny?'

Sam Coulter frowned, not best pleased to have his discussion interrupted by his wife's facetious question.

'Tawny's joie de vivre is without compare, and her face?' Navarre moved his shapely hands with an elegant eloquence that was unmistakeably French. '*Ca suffit…* enough said. How can one quantify such an elusive quality?'

Unexpectedly, Sam gave his wife a fond smile that softened his craggy features. 'I couldn't have said it better myself. The secret of attraction is that it's impossible to put into words.'

Tawny was hardened to her hostess's little gibes by the end of the evening and grateful that other people would be joining them the following day. Catrina might have been married to Sam Coulter for two years but the brunette was very dissatisfied with her life.

Clad in a silk nightdress rather than her usual pjs, for she was making an effort to stay in her role, Tawny climbed into the wide four-poster bed. 'I used to dream of having a bed like this when I was a child,' she said to combat her discomfiture at Navarre's emergence from the bathroom, his tall, well-built physique bare but for a pair of trendy cotton pyjama bottoms.

He looked absolutely spectacular with his black hair spiky with dampness and a faint shadow of stubble highlighting his carved cheekbones and wide, mobile mouth. He also had an amazing set of pecs and obviously worked out regularly. Her attention skimmed over the cluster of dark curls on his torso and the arrowing line of hair bisecting the flat corrugated muscle of his stomach to disappear below his waistband, and her tummy flipped.

'Full marks for all the questions you asked Sam about the history of Strathmore,' Navarre remarked with stunning cynicism. 'He was charmed by your interest.'

Tawny stiffened. 'I wasn't putting on an act. History was my favourite subject next to art and I've always been fascinated by old buildings. Are you always this distrustful of women?'

Brilliant eyes veiled, Navarre shrugged and got into the other side of the bed. 'Let's say that experience has made me wary.'

'Catrina's still keen on you, isn't she? Is that why you wanted a fake fiancée to bring with you?' she asked abruptly.

'One of the reasons,' Navarre conceded evenly. 'And your presence does at least preclude her from making indiscreet remarks.'

Tawny was suffering from an indisputable need to keep on talking to lessen her discomfiture. 'I have to make a phone call some time tomorrow—'

'No,' Navarre responded immediately.

'I'll go behind your back to make the call if you try to prevent me. It's to my grandmother. I always ring her on Saturdays and she'll worry if she doesn't hear from me,' Tawny told him with spirit. 'You can listen to our conversation if you like.'

Navarre punched a pillow and rested his dark head down. 'I'll consider it.'

Tawny flipped round and leant over him. 'See that you do,' she warned combatively.

Navarre reached out and entwined his long brown fingers into the curling spirals of red hair that were brushing his chest. For a timeless moment his eyes held her as fast as manacles. 'Don't tease—'

Her bosom swelled as her temper surged over the rebuke. 'I *wasn't* teasing!'

'You mean that you didn't tell me you were a virgin to whet my appetite for you?' Navarre derided.

'No, I darned well didn't!' Tawny snapped furiously. 'I only told you in the first place because I thought it would make you understand why I was offended by your assumption that my body has a price tag attached to it!'

Navarre was engaged in studying the pulse flickering at the base of the slim column of her throat and the sweet swelling mounds of her breasts visible through the gaping neckline of the nightdress as she bent over him. Hard as a rock, he was still trying to work out what the price tag might encompass so that he could meet the terms and get much better acquainted with that truly exquisite little body of hers.

'I also thought that my inexperience would be more

likely to put you off,' Tawny admitted, her voice trailing away breathily as she connected with his eyes. 'Let go of my hair, Navarre…'

'*Non, ma petite.* I'm enjoying the view too much.'

Only then did Tawny register where his attention was resting and, hot with embarrassment, she lifted the hand she had braced on the pillow by his head to press the neckline of her nightdress flat against her chest.

Navarre laughed with rich appreciation. 'Spoilsport!'

Off-balanced by the rapidity of her own movement, Tawny struggled to pull back from him but he tipped her down instead and encircled her mouth with his own, claiming her full lips with a harsh masculine groan of satisfaction. That sensual mouth on hers was an unimaginable pleasure and it awakened a hunger she could not control. Without her quite knowing how it had happened, she found herself lying back against the pillows with a long masculine thigh pinning her in place. Her hands smoothed over his wide brown shoulders, revelling in the muscles flexing taut below his skin. His fingers flexed over the swell of her breast and her spine arched as his thumb rubbed over the straining nipple. Her response was so powerful that it scared her and she jerked away from him.

'This is not happening!' she gasped in consternation. 'We can't—'

'What do I have to do to make it happen?' Navarre asked huskily.

Tawny tensed and then rolled back, ice blue eyes shooting uncertainly to his face. 'What's that supposed to mean?'

Navarre shifted against her hip, making no attempt to conceal the extent of his arousal. 'Whatever it needs to mean to bring about the desired result, *ma petite*. I want you.'

Tawny flushed and imposed space between them. 'Let's forget about this and go to sleep. I'm working for you. And this situation is exactly why working for you should not include the two of us sharing a bed half naked.'

Navarre toyed with the idea of offering her all the diamonds. Just at that moment no price seemed too high. But that would be treating her like a hooker ready to trade sex for profit. She had got her feelings on that message home, he conceded in growling frustration. He scanned her taut little face and then noticed that she was trembling: there was an almost imperceptible shake in her slight body as she lay there. He compressed his stubborn mouth, rolled back to his own side of the bed and switched out the light. She played hot and then cold but he was beginning to consider the idea that it might not be a deliberate policy to fan his desire to even greater heights. What if she really was a virgin? *As if...*

In the darkness tears inched a slow stinging trail down Tawny's cheeks. She felt out of control and out of her depth and she hated it. She had never understood why people made such a fuss about sex until Navarre had kissed her and if he had tried he probably could have taken her to bed right there and then. Unhappily for him he had missed the boat when she was at her most vulnerable and now she knew that Navarre Cazier somehow had that magical something that reduced her usual defences to rubble. Her breasts ached, the area between her legs seemed to ache as well and even blinking back tears she was within an ace of turning back to him and just surrendering to the powerful forces tormenting her body. Stupid hormones, that was what the problem was!

Tawny was still a virgin purely because the right man

had failed to come along. She had never had a serious relationship, had never known the wild highs and lows of emotional attachment aside of an unrequited crush in her schooldays. She had had several boyfriends at college. There had been loads of kisses and laughs and fun outings but nobody who had made her heart stop with a smile or a kiss. She tensed as Navarre thrust back the sheet with a stifled curse and headed into the bathroom. She listened to the shower running and felt guilty, knowing she had responded, knowing she had encouraged him, but finally deciding that he was not suffering any more from the anticlimax of their lovemaking than she was herself. Restraint physically *hurt*.

Early the following morning she wakened and opened her eyes in the dim room to centre them on Navarre. He was poised at the foot of the bed looking gorgeous and incredibly masculine in shooting clothes that fitted his tall, broad-shouldered and lean-hipped physique so well they were probably tailor made. 'What time is it?' she whispered sleepily.

'Go back to sleep—unless you've changed your mind and decided to come shooting?' As Tawny grimaced at the prospect he laughed softly. *'Peut-être pas*...perhaps not. What was that about you not wanting to kill little fluffy birds, *ma petite*?'

'Not my thing,' she agreed, recalling Sam Coulter's dismay at grouse being given such an emotive description.

'Are you joining us for the shooting lunch?'

'I have no idea. I'll be at Catrina's disposal. She mentioned something about a local spa,' Tawny told him ruefully.

'You'll enjoy that.'

'I hate all that grooming stuff. It's so boring. If I was

here on my own I'd be out horse riding or hiking, doing something active—'

'You can ride?' Navarre made no attempt to hide his surprise.

Watching him intently, Tawny nodded. She decided it was that fabulous bone structure that moved him beyond handsome to stunning. 'My grandparents used to live next door to a riding school and I spent several summers working as a groom.'

Navarre sank down on her side of the bed, stretching out long powerful legs. 'You can phone your grandmother this evening before the party.'

'Thank you.' Her soft pink mouth folded into a blinding smile and he gazed down at her animated face in brooding silence.

Navarre ran a forefinger across the back of the pale hand lying on top of the sheet. 'I've been thinking. I may be willing to extend our association.'

Her brow furrowed. 'Meaning?'

'When our business arrangement is complete I may still want to see you.'

His expression told her nothing and she suppressed the leap of hope inside her that told her more than she wanted to know about her own feelings. 'There's no future in us seeing each other,' she replied flatly.

'When I find it a challenge to stay away from a woman, there is definitely a future, *ma petite*.'

'But that future doesn't extend further than the nearest bed.'

'Don't all affairs begin the same way?' Navarre traded.

And he was *so* right that once again she was tempted to slap him. She didn't want to want him the way she did because such treacherous feelings offended her pride and her intelligence. Yet here she was already imagining how she might lie back in readiness as he pushed aside the sheet and shed his clothes to join her in the bed. Her mind was out of her control. Desire was like a scream buried deep inside her, longing and frantically searching for an escape. Her brain might want to wonder where the relationship could possibly go after fulfillment, but her body cared only that the fulfilment took place.

'Tonight, *ma petite*…I would like to make you mine and you will have no regrets,' Navarre purred, stroking his fingertips delicately along the taut line of her full lower lip, sending wicked little markers of heat travelling to every secret part of her as she thought helplessly of that mouth on hers, those sure, skilled hands, that strong, hard body. She couldn't breathe for excitement.

The shooting lunch was delivered to the men on the moors while those women who had no taste for the sport joined Catrina and Tawny for a more civilised repast at the castle. During that meal, liberally accompanied by fine wine, celebrity and designer names were dropped repeatedly as well as descriptions of fabulous gifts, insanely expensive shopping trips and impossibly luxurious holidays with each woman clearly determined to outdo the next. It was all highly competitive stuff and Tawny hated it, finding the trip to the spa something of a relief, for at least everyone was in separate cubicles and she no longer had to try to fit in by putting on an act.

'You and Navarre won't last,' Catrina informed Tawny confidently as they were driven back to Strathmore.

'Why do you think that?'

'Navarre will get bored and move on, just as he did with me,' Catrina warned. 'I was once in love with him too. I've seen your eyes follow him round the room. When he ditches you, I warn you…it'll hurt like hell.'

'He's not going to ditch me,' Tawny declared between

clenched teeth, wondering if her eyes did follow Navarre round the room. It was an image that mortified her. It was also unnerving that she could be unconscious of her own behaviour around him.

When she entered the bedroom it was a shock to glance through the open bathroom door and see Navarre already standing there naked as he towelled his hair dry. Her face burning, she averted her eyes from that thought-provoking view and went over to the wardrobe to extract the evening dress she planned to wear—a shimmering gold gown that complimented her auburn hair and fair complexion. Her palms were damp. He was gorgeous, stripped he was even more gorgeous. *Tonight...I would like to make you mine.* She shivered at the memory of the words that had burned at the back of her mind throughout the day, full of seductive promise and threatening her self-discipline. For never before had Tawny wanted a man as she wanted Navarre Cazier—with a deep visceral need as primitive as it was fierce.

The towel looped round his narrow hips Navarre strolled out and tossed her mobile phone down on the bed. 'Ring your grandmother,' he told her.

She switched on her phone but there was no reception and after a fruitless moment or two of pacing in an attempt to pick up a signal at the window, Navarre handed her his phone. 'Use mine.'

Celestine answered the call immediately. 'I tried to ring you yesterday but I couldn't get through. I thought you might be too busy to ring, *ma chérie.* And on a Friday evening that would be good news,' the old lady told her chirpily. 'It would mean you had a date which would please me enormously.'

'I am going to a party tonight,' Tawny told her, knowing how much her grandmother would enjoy that news. 'Why were you trying to ring me?'

'A friend of yours called me, said she was trying desperately to get in touch but that you weren't answering your phone. It was that work friend of yours, Julie.'

'Oh…forget about it, it wouldn't have been important.' Tawny felt her skin turn clammy as she wondered what Julie was after now. How dared she disturb her grandmother's peace by phoning her? And where on earth had she got Celestine's number from? It could only have been from Tawny's personnel file, which also meant that Julie had used her computer skills to go snooping again. Had her calculating former friend hoped that the old lady might have information about where Tawny and Navarre had gone after leaving the hotel?

'What are you wearing to the party?' Celestine asked, eager for a description.

And Tawny really pushed the boat out with the details, for the old lady adored finery. Indeed Tawny would have loved to tell Celestine about the Golden Movie Awards and Tia Castelli and her husband, not to mention the castle she was currently staying in, but she did not dare to breathe a word of what Navarre probably considered to be confidential information. Instead she caught up with her grandmother's small daily doings and she slowly began to relax in the reassuring warmth of the old lady's chatter. Unlike her daughter, Susan, Celestine was a very happy personality, who always looked on the bright side of life.

'You seem very close to your grandmother,' Navarre commented as Tawny returned his phone to him.

'She's a darling,' Tawny said fondly, gathering up stuff to take into the en suite with her, mindful of the fact she had been accused of being a tease and determined not to give him further cause to believe that she was actively encouraging his interest.

'What about your mother?'

Tawny paused with her back still turned to him and tried not to wince. 'Relations are a little cool between us at present,' she admitted, opting for honesty.

Mother and daughter were still speaking but things had been said during that last confrontation that would probably never be forgotten, Tawny reflected painfully. Tawny could not forget being told what a drastic disappointment she was to her mother. But then mother and child had always rubbed each other up the wrong way. Tawny had refused to dye her red hair brown when her mother suggested it and had sulked when a padded bra was helpfully presented to her. She had done well in the wrong subjects at school. She had declined to train for a business career and as a result had failed to attain the salary or status that her mother equated with success. And finally and unforgivably on Susan's terms, Tawny had failed to make the most of her entrée into her half-sisters' wealthy world where with some effort she might have met the sort of man her mother would have viewed as an eligible partner. Her recent work as a chambermaid had been the proverbial last straw in her dissatisfied mother's eyes. No, Tawny would never be a daughter whom Susan felt she could boast about with her cronies.

Supressing those unhappy memories of her continuing inability to measure up to parental expectations, Tawny set about doing her make-up. She had watched the make-up artist who had done her face for the Golden Awards carefully and she used eyeliner and gold sparkly shadow with a heavier hand than usual, outlining her lips with a rich strawberry-coloured gloss. The dress had an inner corset for shape and support and she had to breathe in hard and swivel it round to put it on without help. Toting her cosmetic bag, she emerged from the bathroom.

Navarre fell still to look at her and it was one of those very rare occasions when he spoke without forethought. 'Your skin and hair look amazing in that colour.'

'Thank you.' Suddenly shy of him but with a warm feeling coiled up inside her, Tawny turned to the dressing table to put on the diamond earrings and bracelet. Even while she did so she searched out his reflection in the mirror, savouring the sight of him in a contemporary charcoal-grey designer suit. So tall, dark and sophisticated, so wonderfully handsome, Navarre Cazier was the ultimate fantasy male…at that point her thoughts screeched to a sudden stricken halt.

Why was she thinking of him like that? It was past time that she reminded herself that absolutely everything, from the fancy clothes she wore to her supposed relationship with Navarre Cazier, was a giant sham. She felt her upbeat spirits dive bomb. After all, she was not living the fairy tale in a romantic castle with a rich handsome man, she was *faking* it every step of the way. It was a timely recollection.

CHAPTER SIX

Towards midnight, Navarre strode into the ballroom, his keen gaze skimming through the knots of guests until it came to rest on Tawny.

In the subdued light Tawny shimmered like a golden goddess, red hair vibrant, diamonds sparkling, her lovely face full of animation as she looked up at the tall blond man talking to her with a hand clamped to her waist. Navarre recognised her companion immediately: Tor Henson, a wealthy banker very popular with women. Although Navarre had been absent for most of the evening while he talked business with Sam Coulter and had left Tawny very much to her own devices, he was not pleased to see her looking so well entertained. She had not gone without amusement; she had, it seemed, simply *replaced* him. A rare burst of anger ripped through Navarre's big frame, cutting through his powerful self-discipline with disorientating speed and efficiency. His strong white teeth ground together as he crossed the floor to join them.

'*Je suis désolé...*' Navarre began to apologise to Tawny for his prolonged absence.

At the sound of his voice, Tawny whirled round, her expression telegraphing equal amounts of relief and annoyance. 'Where have you been all this time?'

'I gather you don't read the business papers,' Tor Henson

remarked with a knowing glance in Navarre's direction for recent revealing movements on the stock market had hinted that major change could be in store for Sam Coulter's business empire.

Navarre captured a slender white hand in his and held it fast. He wanted to haul her away from Henson and take her upstairs to spread her across their bed, a primal prompting that he dimly understood was born of a rage unlike anything he had ever experienced. 'Thank you for looking after her for me, Tor,' he murmured with glacial courtesy.

'I'm not a child you left behind in need of care and protection!' Tawny objected, ice-blue eyes stormy as he ignored the comment and virtually dragged her onto the dance floor with him. 'Why are you behaving like this, Navarre? Why are you acting like I've done something wrong?'

'Haven't you? If I leave you alone for five minutes I come back to find you flirting with another man!' he censured with icy derision, splaying long sure fingers to her spine to draw her closer to his hard, powerful body than she wanted to be at that moment.

The scent of him, clean, warm and male, was in her nostrils and she fought the aphrodisiac effect that proximity awakened in her treacherous body. 'You left me alone for *two hours*!'

'Was it too much for me to expect you to be waiting quietly where I left you?' Navarre prompted shortly, in no mood to be reasonable.

'Yes, I'm not an umbrella you overlooked and I *wasn't* flirting with Tor! We were simply talking. He knows I'm engaged,' Tawny snapped up at him, tempestuous in her own self-defence.

'Tor would get a kick out of bedding another man's fiancée, *n'est-ce pas*?'

She saw the genuine anger in his gaze and the hard-edged tension in his superb bone structure. 'You're jealous,' she registered in wide-eyed surprise, astonished that she could have that much power over him.

His beautiful mouth took on a contemptuous curve. 'Of course I'm not jealous. Why would I be jealous? We're not really engaged,' he reminded her very drily.

But Tawny was not so easily deflected from an opinion once she had formed it. 'Maybe you're naturally the possessive type in relationships... You definitely didn't like seeing me enjoy myself in another man's company. But have you any idea how insulting it is for you to insinuate that I might go off and shag some guy I hardly know?'

'I'd have bedded you within five minutes of meeting you, *ma petite*,' Navarre confided with a roughened edge to his voice, holding her so close to his body that she could feel the effect her closeness was having on him and warmth pooled in the pit of her tummy in response to his urgent male sexuality.

'I'm not like you—I would never have agreed to that!' Tawny proclaimed heatedly, stretching up on tiptoe to deliver that news as close to his ear as she could reach.

'*Mais non*...I can be very persuasive.' Navarre laced long deft fingers into her tumbling curls to hold her steady while he bent his mouth to hers, his breath fanning her cheek. He was no fan of public displays but in that instant he was controlled by a driving atavistic need to mark her as his so that no other man would dare to approach her again. He crushed her succulent lips apart and tasted her with uninhibited hunger, not once but over and over again until she shuddered against him, her slight body vibrating like a tuning fork in response to his passion.

With reluctance, Navarre dragged his mouth from hers, scanned her rapt face and urged her towards the exit. 'Let's go.'

Go where? she almost asked, even though she knew where. She could not find the breath or the will to argue. After all, she *wanted* to be alone with him. She wanted him to kiss her again, she had never wanted anything more, and where once the presence of others might have acted as a welcome control exercise, this time around it was an annoyance. Objections lay low in the back of her mind, crushed out of existence by the fierce longing rippling through her in seductive waves.

'This has to be a beginning, not an end,' Navarre declared, thrusting shut the door of the bedroom.

Tawny didn't want him to talk, she only wanted him to kiss her. As long as he was kissing her she didn't have to think and wonder about whether or not she was making a mistake. Even worse, the wanting was so visceral that she could not stand against the force of it.

He unzipped her gown, ran his fingers smoothly down her slender spine and flipped loose her bra. She shivered, electrified with anticipation, knees turning to water as his hands rose to cup the swelling mounds of her breasts and massage the achingly sensitive nipples. He touched her exactly as she wanted to be touched. She had never dreamt that desire might leave her so weak that it was a challenge to stay upright, but now as she leant back against him and struggled simply to get oxygen into her lungs she was learning the lesson. She turned round in the circle of his arms and kissed him, hands closing into his jacket and pushing it off his broad shoulders. For an instant he stepped back, shedding the jacket, freeing his shirt from his waistband to unbutton it.

Just looking at him made her mouth run dry. A muscular bronzed section of hair-roughened torso was visible between the parted edges of his shirt and she wanted to touch, explore, *taste*...it was as though he had got under her skin and changed her from inside out, teaching her to crave what she had never even thought of before. Now she didn't just think, she acted. She raised her hands to that hard flat abdomen and let her palms glide up over the corrugated muscles to discover the warm skin and revel shamelessly in the way that her touch made him tense and roughly snatch his breath in.

Navarre lifted her free of her gown and she stood there, feeling alarmingly naked in only her high heels and a flimsy pair of white silk knickers. He sank down on the side of the bed and drew her down between his spread thighs, nibbling sensuously at her swollen lower lip while he eased his hand beneath the silk and rubbed the most sensitive spot of all with a skill and rhythm that provoked a series of gasps from her throat.

'I want you naked, *ma petite*...' he breathed thickly as he slid down her knickers and removed them, flipping off her shoes with the careless casual skill of a man practised at undressing women. 'And then I want you every way I can have you.'

Navarre bent her back over his arm and brought his mouth down hungrily on the proud pouting tip of an engorged nipple, drawing on the sensitised bud while his hand continued to explore the most sensitive part of her. Her fingers dug into his black cropped hair as he caressed her, a sharp arrow of need slivering through her. 'You're wearing too many clothes,' she told him shakily.

He settled her down on the bed and stood over her stripping. The shirt and the trousers were followed by his boxers. She had never seen a man naked and aroused before and she couldn't take her eyes off the long thick steel of his bold length. She was both intimidated and aroused by the size of him. Her face hot with self-consciousness, she scrabbled below the covers, her entire body tingling with extra-sensory awareness. He tossed foil-wrapped condoms down on top of the bedside cabinet and slid in beside her, so hot and hard and strong that he sent a wave of energising desire through her the instant she came into contact with his very male physique.

He detached the diamond earrings still dangling from her ears and set them aside, brilliant green eyes locked to her anxious face. 'What's wrong?'

As he leant down to her she closed her arms round his neck and kissed him, needing the oblivion of passion to feel secure, trembling as the hot hardness of his muscular body connected with hers. He lowered his tousled dark head and kissed her breasts, teasing her straining nipples with his tongue and pulling on the oversensitive buds until her hips squirmed in frustration on the mattress. Only then did he touch her where she most needed to be touched. He explored the silken warmth between her thighs with deft fingers and then he subjected that tender flesh to his mouth. She was unprepared for that ultimate intimacy and she jerked away in shock and tried to withdraw from it, but he closed his hands on her hips and held her fast until sensation spread like wildfire at the heart of her and entrapped her as surely as a prison cell. She wanted more of that wild, intoxicating feeling, she couldn't help wanting *more;* she was a slave to sensation. The hunger rose like a great white roar inside her, bypassing her every attempt to control it. Her body was shaking and the constricted knot at her core was notching tighter and tighter until the pleasure just rose in a huge overwhelming tide and engulfed her, leaving her shuddering and crying out in reaction.

'Navarre…' she whispered jaggedly.

'You liked that, *ma petite*,' he husked with all the satisfaction of a man who knew he had given a woman unimaginable pleasure.

Numbly she nodded, every reaction slowed down. It had never occurred to her that her body could feel anything that intensely and in the stunned aftermath of that climax she was only dimly aware that he was reaching for a condom, and then he was reaching for her again. Her body was pliant with obedience, already trained to expect pleasure from him, and as he pushed back her thighs and rose over her she quivered with the awareness of him hard and bold and alien at her tiny entrance, but there was a sense of trust as well.

'You're so tight,' he groaned with pleasure as he sank into her tender channel with controlled care.

A startled sound somewhere between a gasp and a cry was wrenched from her as he broke through the fragile barrier of her inexperience. Her body flinched and he stilled in the act of possession, staring down at her with scorching green eyes fringed by black, recognising in that heightened instant of awareness that he was the only lover she had ever had. 'You were telling me the truth…'

'Women aren't all liars,' Tawny breathed, shuddering as he drove all the way home to the heart of her body.

Immersed in the molten heat of her, Navarre was fighting for control, leaning down to crush her mouth under his again and breathe in the luscious scent of her skin. She felt so good, she smelt even better. He shifted his lean hips and thrust, wanting to take it slow and easy but struggling against his explosive level of arousal with every second that passed. Tawny arched up into him with a whimper of encouragement and he sank deeper, harder and suddenly he couldn't hold back any more against the elemental storm of need riding him. Holding her firmly, he eased back until he had almost withdrawn and then he thrust back into her with seductive force. The pleasure was building inside Tawny again in a wild surge of sensation that scooped her up and left her defenceless. His provocative rhythm heightened every feeling to an unbearable level and then all of a sudden it was as if a blinding white light exploded inside her, heat and hunger coalescing in a fierce fiery orgasm.

In the heady, dizzy aftermath she thought she might never move again, for her limbs felt weighted to the bed. She was incredibly grateful that she had chosen him as her lover, for he had made it extraordinary and she knew that was rare for a first experience. She hugged him tight, pressed her lips to a smooth brown shoulder, able to reason in only the most simplistic of ways, her brain on shutdown. He rolled back from her and headed for the bathroom.

It crossed her mind that barely a week earlier he had been a billionaire businessman and hotel guest to her. Now what was he? A very desirable lover who could also be absolutely infuriating and the guy who was *paying* her to fake being his fiancée. As cruel reality kicked in Tawny flinched from it, alarmed that she could have forgotten the financial nature of their agreement. It was a complication, but not one that couldn't be handled with the right attitude on both sides, she reasoned frantically, determined to stay optimistic rather than lash herself with pointless regrets. What was done was done. He was her lover now.

Navarre reappeared from the bathroom and strolled back to the bed. She had fallen sound asleep, a tangle of rich red curls lying partially across her perfect profile, a hand tucked childishly below her cheek. That fast he wanted her again and the strength of that desire disturbed him. Desire was wonderful as long as it stayed within certain acceptable bounds. Uninhibited hunger that threatened his control was not his style at all, for it was more likely to add complications to a life he preferred to keep smooth and untrammelled, a soothing contrast to his troubled and changeable childhood years. At heart he would always be an unrepentant loner and he thought it unlikely that he would change, for everything from his birth to his challenging adolescence had conspired to make him what he was. He had seduced her, though, he knew he had, and taking her virginity had roused the strangest protective instinct inside him. Even so he was equally aware that he could not afford to forget that she was a thief whose loyalty was for sale to the highest bidder...

Tawny wakened while it was still dark, immediately conscious of the new tenderness between her thighs and the ache of unfamiliar muscles. Instantly memory flooded back and she slid quiet as a wraith from the bed, padding across the carpet to the bathroom. Although it was almost four in the morning she ran a warm bath and settled into the soothing water to hug her knees and regroup. She had slept with Navarre Cazier and it had been amazing.

She didn't want to get all introspective and female about what had happened between them, for common sense told her that such powerful physical attraction as theirs generally only led to one conclusion. She especially didn't want to think about the feelings he was beginning to awaken inside her: the stab of intense satisfaction she had felt once she had registered that he was jealous of that banker's interest in her, the sense of achievement when he listened to her and laughed, the walking-on-air sensation when he admired her appearance, her unreserved delight in discovering that unashamed passion of his, which was so at variance with his cool, unemotional façade.

She knew without being told that she was walking a dangerous line. She had abandoned her defences and taken the kind of risk she had never taken before. Yet wouldn't she do it again given the chance to feel what he had made her feel? It wasn't just physical either. It was more that astonishing sense of feeling insanely alive for the first time ever, that wondrous sense of connection to another human being. Still lost in her thoughts, Tawny patted herself dry with a fleecy towel. She decided that she wasn't going to act the coward and bail on the experience just because it was unlikely to give her a happy ending. She was only twenty-three years old, she reminded herself doggedly, way too young to be worrying about needing a happy ending with a man. She tiptoed back to bed, eased below the cool sheets, and when a long masculine arm stretched out as though to retrieve her and tugged her close she went willingly into that embrace.

She loved the scent of his skin, clean and male laced with an evocative hint of designer cologne. She breathed in that already familiar scent as though it were an addictive drug, her fingers fanning out across his flat stomach as she shifted position. She adored being so close to him because she was very much aware that when he was awake he was not a physically or verbally demonstrative man likely to make her feel secure with displays of affection or appreciation. Her hand smoothed possessively down a hair-roughened thigh and he released a drowsy groan of approval.

In the darkness a cheeky smile curved her generous mouth when she discovered that even asleep he was aroused and ready for action. Wide awake now and unashamedly keen to experiment she became a little more daring and her fingertips carefully traced the steely length of his shaft. With a muffled sound of appreciation Navarre shifted position and began to carry out his own reconnaissance. She was stunned by how fast her body reacted to his sleepy caresses with her nipples stiffening into instant tingling life while heat and moisture surged between her legs. Muttering a driven French imprecation, he pinned her beneath him, his hands suddenly hard with urgency as he pushed between her slender thighs and drove hungrily into her yielding body again. Instinctively she arched up to him to ease the angle of his entrance and he ground his body deeper into hers with a guttural sound of pleasure. He moved slowly and provocatively in a strong sensual rhythm. Her lips parted as she breathed in urgent gasps, clinging to his broad shoulders as the glorious pressure began to build and build within her. She came apart in an explosive climax as his magnificent body shuddered to the same crest with her. A glorious tide of exquisite sensation cascaded through her spent body.

In an abrupt movement, Navarre freed himself of her hands and rolled away from her to switch on the lights. Blinded by the sudden illumination, Tawny blinked in bewilderment.

'*Merde alors!* Was this a planned seduction?' Navarre flung at her furiously, a powerfully intimidating figure against the pale bedding as she peered at him from narrowed eyes. 'To be followed by a meticulously planned conception?'

Utterly bemused by that accusation, Tawny pushed herself up against the tumbled pillows with frantic hands. 'What on earth are you talking about? Seduction, for heaven's sake?'

'We just had sex without a condom!' Navarre fired at her in condemnation.

'Oh…my…goodness,' Tawny framed in sudden comprehension, her skin turning clammy in shock. 'I didn't think of that—'

'Didn't you? You woke me out of a sound sleep to make love to you. A lot of men would overlook precautions in the excitement of the moment!'

'You can't seriously think I deliberately tempted you into sex while you were half asleep in the hope that you would forget to use a condom?' Tawny told him roundly, colour burnishing her cheeks.

'Why wouldn't I think that? I once caught a woman in the act of puncturing a condom in the hope of conceiving a child without my knowledge!' Navarre ground out in contemptuous rebuttal. 'Why should you be any different? Wealthy men are always targets for a fertile woman. When a man fathers a child by a woman he's bound to support her and her offspring for a couple of decades!'

'I feel sorry for you,' Tawny breathed tightly, her small face stony with self-control. 'It must be crippling to be as suspicious of other human beings as you are. Everybody is not out to con you or make money out of you, Navarre!'

'I've already caught you thieving from me,' Navarre reminded her icily. 'So forgive me for not being impressed by your claim to be morally superior.'

In the wake of that exchange, Tawny had lost every scrap of her natural colour. She had not required that final lowering reminder of how she had attempted to make off with his laptop. Lying there naked with her body still damp and aching from his lovemaking, she felt like the worst kind of whore. He had to despise her to be so suspicious of her motives that even an act of lovemaking could be regarded as a potential attempt to rip him off. It was a brutal wake-up call to the reality that, while she had moved on from the humiliation of their first meeting, his opinion of her was still that of a calculating little thief without morals. Sleeping with her had not changed his outlook and what a fool she had been to believe otherwise. Had he really caught a woman damaging contraception in the hope of falling pregnant by him? She was appalled. No wonder he was such a cynic if that was the sort of woman he was accustomed to having in his bed.

'We'll discuss this tomorrow,' Navarre breathed curtly as he doused the lights again.

'Let's not,' she said woodenly, turning on her side so that her back was turned to him. 'My system's very irregular—I'm pretty sure we won't have anything to worry about.'

But in spite of that breezy assurance she was still lying wide awake and worrying long after the deep even sound of his breathing had alerted her to the fact that he had gone back to sleep. Why, oh, why had she chosen to overlook the fact that he was paying her thousands of pounds to pretend to be his fiancée? Money problems always changed the nature of relationships, she thought wretchedly. The cash angle had put a wall between them. It was the single biggest difference between them, that reminder that he was rich and she was poor, never mind the truth that he had found her apparently stealing from him. Why had she believed that she could handle sex in such an unequal relationship? He had just proven how wrong that conviction could be.

By the time that dawn was lightening the darkness behind the curtains, Tawny had had enough of lying in the bed as still as a corpse. She got up again as quietly as she could and decided that she could go out for a walk without disturbing the entire household. The only clothes of her own that she had packed were her skinny jeans and skeleton tee. She put them on, teaming them with a woollen jacket with a velvet collar and a pair of laced boots. She crept out of the room and downstairs and was soon out in the fresh air experiencing a deep abiding sense of relief and a desperate need to reclaim her freedom.

The charade of their engagement would shortly be over, she told herself soothingly. Soon she would be back home and out searching for another job. Hopefully the turmoil of overexcited feelings that she was currently feeling would vanish along with Navarre Cazier...

CHAPTER SEVEN

'TAWNY! I saw you walking up the drive from the window. Navarre will be relieved—he's been looking everywhere for you!' Catrina told her brightly as Tawny mounted the front steps, muddy and windblown and embarrassed by her long absence and untidy appearance. It occurred to her that her hostess had never smiled at her with such welcoming warmth before but she was in too troubled a state of mind to be suspicious.

'I went out for a walk and got a bit lost,' Tawny muttered apologetically. 'Have I missed breakfast?'

'No. Navarre was worried that you had seen that story in the newspapers and been upset by it…it's so embarrassing when these things happen when you're away from home,' Catrina commented with unconvincing sympathy.

Tawny had frozen in the hallway. 'What newspaper story?'

Catrina helpfully passed her the tabloid newspaper she was already clutching in readiness. 'I'll have breakfast sent up to your room if you like.'

Tawny opened the paper and there it was: *Billionaire and Maid?* There was a beaming picture of Julie, her self-elected best friend, who she could only assume had spilled her guts to a reporter for cash. She supposed that in the absence of any more colourful story about Navarre going with an engagement that had to be a fake must have seemed worthwhile. Almost everything she had ever told Julie that could be given the right twist was there in black and white from Tawny's brief time in foster care as a child to the recent mysterious breakdown in family relations. Oh, yes, *and* what Julie described as Tawny's frantic determination to meet and marry a rich man through her work...*yes,* Julie had had to find an angle to make Tawny sound more interesting and that was the angle she had chosen. Tawny was a rampant gold-digger in search of a meal ticket. According to Julie Tawny had used her employment as a chambermaid to sleep with several wealthy guests in a search for one who would offer to take her away from cleaning and spoil her to death with his money for ever. What insane rubbish! Tawny thought furiously, wondering who on earth would believe such nonsense.

'Wouldn't you prefer to have your breakfast in your room?' Catrina Coulter prompted expectantly.

'Have all the guests seen this?' Tawny enquired.

Catrina gave her a sympathetic glance as unconvincing as her earlier smile. 'Probably...'

'I'll be eating downstairs,' Tawny announced, folding the paper and tucking it casually below one arm to march into the lofty-ceilinged dining room with her bright head held high and a martial glint in her gaze. A moment too late she recalled that her hair was in a wild tangle and her jeans spattered with mud, but she had to tough out that knowledge because her fellow guests turned as one to watch her progress down the length of the long table towards the empty chair beside Navarre.

Navarre, sleek and sexy in a striped shirt and a pair of designer chinos, stood up as she approached and spun out the chair for her. Inside, her body hummed as if an engine had been switched on. Her eyes, with an alacrity all their own, darted over him, taking in the cropped black hair, the brilliant green eyes and the dark shadow that told her he hadn't shaved since the night before. And it was no use, in spite of the fact that she was furious with him the fact that he was drop-dead gorgeous triumphed and she blushed with awareness, her heartbeat quickening in time with her pulse as she sank down into the seat.

'I'll get you something to eat,' Navarre offered, vaulting upright to stride across to the side table laden with lidded dishes laid out on hot plates for guests to serve themselves.

Surprised that he was giving her that amount of attention, Tawny watched him heap a dining plate as high as if he were feeding half the table instead of just one skinny redhead and bring it back to her with positive ceremony.

'You must've walked miles...you have to be starving,' he pointed out when she gaped at the amount of food he had put on the plate.

Trying not to laugh at the shocked appraisal of the blonde with a health conscious plate of fresh fruit opposite, Tawny began to butter her first slice of toast. 'I walked miles more than I planned. I'm afraid I found myself on boggy ground and got lost and very muddy. I ended up having to walk along the road to find my way back here. I shouldn't have gone so far without a map,' she confided breathlessly as he poured her coffee for her.

Tawny sugared her coffee while wondering why Navarre, who had hurt her so much just hours earlier, was now being so kind and attentive. Had he not read the same newspaper spread? Didn't he realise that she could only have tried to steal his laptop to grab his attention and then bonk his brains out in the hope that great sex would make him her meal ticket for life? It was obvious that the rest of the guests had read the newspaper. She was painfully conscious that everyone else at the table was watching her and Navarre closely, clearly hoping for some gossipy titbit or some sign that he was going to dump her right there and then. Thanks to her erstwhile friend she had been depicted in print as a mercenary chambermaid who had seduced innocent hotel guests in an effort to entrap a wealthy husband.

Navarre watched Tawny eat a cooked breakfast with the enthusiasm of a woman who had not seen food for a month. He was relieved to see that a scurrilous article in a downmarket newspaper had not detracted from her appetite. Above all things Navarre admired courage and the courage she had displayed in choosing to take her breakfast as normal in front of an inquisitive audience hugely impressed him. Few women would have kept their cool in such an embarrassing situation.

'I have to pack,' she told him prosaically once she had finished her second cup of coffee.

In the mood Tawny was in the packing did not take long. Ten minutes and it was done. Navarre walked into the room just as she lowered the case to the floor. She would have offered to do his packing as well just to keep busy but he had already taken care of the task. She folded her arms defensively.

'We should talk before the helicopter arrives,' Navarre imparted flatly. 'We'll be staying in another hotel for the next couple of days, after which I will let you return to your life. I'll be tied up with business once we return to London.'

Tawny said nothing. Another hotel, mercifully not the one where she had once been employed. It was clear that their arrangement would soon have run its course. So much for his declaration the night before that their intimacy was to be a beginning and not an end! She had fallen for a line, it seemed.

Navarre studied her with sardonic cool. 'I hope you won't prove to be pregnant.'

Tawny stiffened. 'I hope so too, particularly because it would be my life which would be majorly screwed up by that development.'

'It would screw up *both* our lives,' Navarre countered grimly.

Tawny resisted the urge to challenge that statement. She was too well aware as a child born to a single mother that her birth had made little impact on her own father's life. Monty Blake had paid the court-ordered minimum towards Tawny's upkeep and that was all. He had not taken an interest in her. He had not invited her to visit him, his second wife and their family. Indeed he had deliberately excluded Tawny from family occasions. When her mother had chosen to continue her pregnancy against his wishes he had hit back by doing everything he could to ignore Tawny's existence. Had her older half-sisters not chosen to look her up when she was a teenaged schoolgirl, Tawny would never have got to know them either. Certainly she would never have had the confidence to approach either Bee or Zara on her own behalf when their father had made her feel so very unworthy of his affection. And that hurtful feeling of not being good enough to be an acceptable daughter had dogged her all her life.

That evening, Tawny was once again ensconced in a hotel suite with only Elise for company. Navarre had chatted at length in Italian to someone on the phone while the car travelled slowly through the London traffic and as soon as they checked into the hotel he had gone out again. This time around, however, the suite Navarre had taken had *two* bedrooms. She was not expected to sleep on the sofa or share his bed. Their little fling was over. She reminded herself of the unjust accusation he had made before dawn that same day, relived her fury and hurt at that charge and told herself that it was only sensible to avoid further intimacy and misunderstanding. While Elise watched television Tawny worked through her emotions with the help of her sketch pad, drawing little cartoon vignettes of her rocky relationship with Navarre.

Navarre came back just after midnight, exchanging a word or two with Elise as she raised herself sleepily from the sofa, switched off the television and bid him goodnight. Left alone, he lifted Tawny's sketch pad. The Frenchman, it said on the first page, and there he was in all his cartoon glory, leching at the stylist while pretending to admire Tawny in her evening dress. He leafed through page after page of caricatures and laughter shook him, for she had a quirky sense of humour and he could only hope that the one depicting Catrina as a man-eating piranha fish never made it into the public eye, for Sam would be mortally offended at the insult to his wife. His supreme indifference to the newspaper revelations about her background as a maid was immortalised in print as she showed him choosing to fret instead about how much fried food the English ate at breakfast time. Did she really see him as that insensitive? Admittedly he avoided getting up close and personal on an emotional front with women, for time and experience had taught him that that was unwise if he had no long-term intentions.

'Oh, you're back...' Tawny emerged from her bedroom, clad in her pyjamas, which had little monkeys etched all over the trousers and a big monkey on the front of the camisole, none of which detracted in the slightest from his awareness of the firm swell of her breasts and the lush prominence of her nipples pushing against the thin clinging cotton. 'I'm thirsty.'

He watched as she padded drowsily over to the kitchenette in one corner to run the cold tap and extract a glass from a cupboard. He was entranced by the smallness of her waist and the generous fullness of her derriere beneath the cotton: she was *all* woman in the curve department in spite of her slender build. His groin tightened as he remembered the feel of her hips in his hands and the hot tight grip of her beneath him. He crushed that lingering memory, fought to rise above it and concentrate instead on the divisive issues that kept his desire within acceptable boundaries.

'Why did you take my laptop that day?' he demanded without warning.

Tawny almost dropped the moisture-beaded glass she was holding. 'I told you why. I thought you'd taken nude photos of my friend and refused to delete them. She told me that if I got it for her she would wipe them. I believed her—at the time I trusted her as a good friend but I realised afterwards that she was lying to me and hoping to make money out of it. She was working for a journalist who wanted information on you and your activities.'

'I know,' Navarre volunteered, startling her. 'I had Julie checked out—'

'And you didn't think to mention that to me?'

'I have no proof that you weren't in it for a profit with her, *ma petite*.'

'No, obviously I would think that it would be much more profitable to get pregnant with a child you don't want so that I could be lumbered with its sole care for the next twenty years!' Tawny sizzled back.

'I didn't realise that you'd once been in a foster home as well,' Navarre remarked, carefully sidestepping her emotive comeback, believing it to be the wrong time for that conversation. 'You didn't mention it when I admitted my own experiences.'

'Obviously you read every line of that newspaper article,' Tawny snapped defensively. 'But I was only in foster care for a few months and as soon as my grandparents found out where I was they offered to take me. When I was a toddler my mother hit a rough patch when she was drinking too much and I was put into care. But she overcame her problems so that I was able to live with her again.'

'Clearly you respect your mother for that achievement, so why are you at odds with her now?'

At that blunt question, Tawny paled, for the newspaper article had not clarified that situation. 'My grandfather's will,' she explained with a rueful jerk of a slim shoulder that betrayed her eagerness to forget that unpleasant reality. 'My grandparents owned and lived in a cottage in a village where my grandmother was very happy. When my grandfather died he left half of it to his wife and the other half to his only child, my mother. My mother made my grandmother sell her home so that she could collect on her share.'

Navarre was frowning. 'And you disapproved?'

'Of course I did. My grandmother was devastated by the loss of her home so soon after she had lost her husband. It was cruel. I understood that my mother has always had a struggle to survive and had never owned her own home but I still think what she did was wrong. I tried to dissuade her from forcing Gran to sell up but she wouldn't listen. Her boyfriend had more influence over her than I had,' Tawny admitted unhappily. 'As far as Mum was concerned Grandad might have been Gran's husband but he had also been her father and she had rights too. She put her own rights first, so the house was sold and Gran, who had always been so good to us both, moved into a retirement village where—I have to admit—she's quite happy.'

'Your mother gave way to temptation and she has to live with that. At least your grandmother had sufficient funds left after the division of property to move somewhere she liked.'

Tawny said nothing. She had seen no sign that her mother was suffering from an uneasy conscience and, having put all that she possessed into purchasing her new apartment, Celestine's current lifestyle was seriously underfunded. But Tawny believed that subjecting the old lady to the stress of changing to more affordable accommodation would be downright dangerous, for Celestine had already suffered one heart attack. The upheaval of another house move might well kill her.

'I'd better get back to bed.' But instead Tawny hovered, her gaze welded to the stunning eyes above his well-defined cheekbones, the beautiful wilful line of his passionate mouth.

'I want to go there with you, *ma petite,*' Navarre admitted in his dark, distinctively accented drawl.

As if a naked flame had burned her skin, Tawny spun on her heel and went straight back into her bedroom, closing the door with a definitive little snap behind her. She flung herself back below the duvet, tears of frustration stinging her eyes, her body switching onto all systems go at the very thought of him in the same bed again. Stupid, silly woman that she was, she craved the chance to be with him again!

Navarre had just emerged from a long cooling shower when Tia phoned him. She wanted him to bring Tawny to a weekend party she and Luke were staging on a yacht in the Med. He rarely said no to the beautiful actress but he said it this time, knowing that it would be wiser to sever all ties with his pretend fiancée rather than draw her deeper into Tia's glitzy world. Mixing business, pleasure and dark secrets could not work for long. He would pay Tawny for her time and draw a line under the episode: it was the safest option. He refused to consider the possibility that she might fall pregnant. If it happened he would deal with it, but he wouldn't lose sleep worrying about it beforehand.

Navarre had left the hotel by the time Tawny was ready for breakfast the next morning. She was bored silly and not even her sketch pad could prevent her from feeling restless. 'Where's your boss?' she pressed Elise.

'He's in business meetings all day,' the blonde confided. 'We're returning home tomorrow…I can't wait.'

'You'll see your boyfriend,' Tawny gathered, reckoning that it had to be the strongest sign yet of her unimportance on Navarre's scale that even his employees knew he was leaving the UK before she did.

But life would soon return to normal, she told herself firmly. She had had a one-night stand and she wasn't very proud of the fact. The next day, however, she would be out job-hunting again as well as getting in touch with her agent to see if she had picked up any new illustrating commissions. She would also catch the train down to visit Celestine at the weekend. Elise got her the local papers so that she could study the jobs available and she decided to look for a waitressing position rather than applying to become a maid again. A waitress would have more customer contact. It would be livelier, more demanding, and wasn't distraction exactly what her troubled mind needed?

No way did she need to be wondering how she would cope if she had conceived a child by Navarre! There was even less excuse for her to be wondering whether she would prefer a boy or a girl and whether the baby might look like her or take more after Navarre, with his dramatic black hair and green eyes. If she turned out to be pregnant, she had no doubt that she would have much more serious concerns. Her mother had once admitted that she had been thrilled when she first realised that she was carrying Tawny. Back then, of course, Susan Baxter had naively assumed that a child on the way would cement her relationship with her child's father instead of which it had destroyed it. At least, Tawny reflected ruefully, she cherished no such romantic illusions where Navarre Cazier was concerned.

About ten that evening, Tawny ran a bath to soak in and emerged pink and wrinkled from her submersion, engulfed in the folds of a large hotel dressing gown. At that point and quite unexpectedly, for Elise had believed him out for the evening, Navarre strode in, clad in a dark, faultlessly tailored business suit with a heavy growth of stubble darkening his handsome features. He acknowledged Elise with barely a glance, for his attention remained on Tawny with her vibrant curls rioting untidily round her flushed face and her slender body lost in the depths of the oversized robe she wore. Hunger pierced him as sharply as a knife, a hunger he didn't understand because it had not started at the groin. That lingering annoying sense that something was lacking, something lost, infuriated him on a day when he had more reason than most to be in an excellent mood to celebrate. He was the triumphant new owner of CCC. The deal had been agreed at Strathmore after weeks of pre-contract discussions between their lawyers and various consultants and now it was signed, sealed and delivered.

'Goodnight, Navarre,' Tawny said flatly.

Elise slipped out of the door unnoticed by either of them. 'I'm leaving tomorrow,' he told Tawny without any expression at all.

Tawny smiled as brightly as if she had won an Olympic race. 'Elise mentioned it.'

'I'll drop you off at home on the way to the airport. I have your phone number and I'll stay in touch...obviously,' he added curtly.

'It's not going to happen,' Tawny responded soothingly, guessing what he meant. 'My egg and your sperm are more likely to have a fight than get together and throw a party for three!'

His face darkened. 'I hope you're right, *ma petite*. A child should be planned and wanted and cherished.'

Her eyes stung as she thought of how much truth there was in that statement. Her own life might have been very different had her parents respected that example. Struggling to suppress the over emotional tears threatening, she was only capable of nodding agreement, but she was grateful that he wasn't approaching the thorny subject with hypocrisy or polite and empty lies. He didn't want to have a child with her and she appreciated his honesty. She shed the robe and got into bed where the tears simply overflowed. She sniffed and coughed, furious with herself. He might have lousy square taste in women's clothes, but he was fantastic in bed and that was the *sole* source of her regret where Navarre Cazier was concerned. He would have made a great casual lover, she told herself doggedly, refusing to examine her feelings in any greater depth.

About twenty minutes later, a light knock sounded on her door and she called out, 'Come in!' and sat up to put on the light by the bed.

She was stunned when Navarre appeared in the doorway, his only covering a towel loosely knotted round his narrow hips. 'May I stay with you tonight?'

Her mouth ran dry, her throat closed over, but her body

went off on a roller-coaster ride of instant sit-up-and-beg response. 'Er…'

'I've tried but I can't stop wanting you,' Navarre admitted harshly.

And she admired that frankness and the streak of humility it had taken for him to approach her again after he had attempted to close that door and move their relationship into more platonic channels. He was not so different from her, after all, and it was a realisation that softened her resentment when she couldn't stop wanting him either. 'Stay,' she told him gruffly, switching out the light in the hope it would hide her discomfiture.

That she was too weak to send him packing still offended Tawny's pride. He had suspected that she might be in league with Julie to plunder his life for profitable information that could be sold to the press. He even believed she might have deliberately tried to get pregnant by him because he was a wealthy man. He did not see her as a trustworthy woman with moral scruples. He was rich, she was poor and a gulf of suspicion separated them. She ought to hate him, but when the muscle packed heat and power of Navarre eased up against her in the dimness, a healthy dose of blood cooling hatred was nowhere to be found. Instead a snaking coil of heat uncurled and burned hot in her and she quivered, every nerve ending energised by anticipation.

Navarre had spent the day in an ever more painful state of arousal, which had steadily eaten away at his self-discipline. Throughout he had remained hugely aware that this was the last night he could be with Tawny and the temptation of having her so close had finally overpowered every other consideration. He might be violating his principles, but when had he ever pretended that he was perfect? In any case, he reasoned impatiently, sex was just sex and it would be an even worse mistake to get emotional about a wholly physical prompting. She turned him on hard and fast, she had made sex exciting for him again. What was a moral dilemma in comparison to what she could make him feel?

Having divided his attention hungrily between the large pink nipples that adorned her small firm breasts and discovered that she was even more deliciously responsive than he recalled, Navarre slowly worked his way down her slender body, utilising every expert skill he had ever learned in the bedroom. If she could make him want her to such an extent, that power had to cut both ways and he was not content until she was writhing and whimpering in abandon, pleading for that final fix of fulfilment.

He sank deep into her and an aching wave of pleasure engulfed her, the little shivers and shakes of yet another approaching climax overwhelming her until she was sobbing out her satisfaction into a hard brown shoulder and falling back against the pillows again, weak as a kitten, emptied of everything.

Still struggling to recapture his breath after that wild bout of sex, Navarre threw himself back out of the bed before he could succumb to the need to reach for her again. Once was never enough with her, but he was suddenly in the grip of a fierce need to prove to himself that he *could* turn away from the powerful temptation she offered. In the darkness he searched for his towel in the heap of clothing discarded by the bed. He shook a couple of garments with unconcealed impatience and Tawny stretched up to put on the bedside light.

'Where are you going?' Clutching the sheet to her chest, frowning below the tumbled curls on her brow, Tawny studied him, unable to believe that he could already be leaving her again. A quick tumble and that was that? Was that all the consideration he now had for her? Did familiarity breed contempt that fast?

Navarre snatched up the towel and at the same time what he took for a screwed up banknote on the floor, assuming it had fallen out of an item of her clothing when he shook it. As he smoothed the item out to give it to her he caught a glimpse of his own name and he withdrew his hand and stepped back from the bed to read the block printed words on the piece of paper.

'If you call…' the note ran and a London phone number followed. 'Information about Navarre Cazier is worth a lot of money.'

Seeing that scrap of paper in his hand, Tawny almost had a heart attack on the spot and she lunged towards him with a stricken gasp. 'Give me that!'

His face set like a mask, Navarre crumpled the note in a powerful fist and dropped it down on her lap. '*Merde alors!* What information about me are you planning to sell?' he enquired silkily.

After their intimacy mere minutes earlier it was like a punch in the stomach for Tawny to be asked that brutal question. He had simply assumed that, in spite of the fact that he had already offered her a very large sum of money to help him out, she would think nothing of going behind his back to the press and selling confidential information about him. It was a blow that Navarre could still think so little of her morals. She lost so much colour that her hair looked unnaturally bright against her pallor.

'News of my successful buyout of CCC was in the evening papers so you've missed the boat on the business front,' Navarre derided, winding the towel round his narrow hips with apparently calm hands. 'What else have you got to sell?'

Tawny breathed in deep and gave him a wide sizzling

smile that hurt lips still swollen from his kisses. 'Basically the story of what you're like in bed. You know, the usual sleaze that makes up a kiss-and-tell, how you treated me like a royal princess and put a ring on my finger for a few days, had the sex and then got bored and dumped me again.'

Still as a bronzed statue, Navarre focused contemptuous green eyes on her and ground out the reminder, 'You signed a confidentiality agreement.'

'I know I did, but somehow I don't think you'll lower yourself to the task of dragging me into a courtroom just because I tell the world that you're a five-times-a night guy!' Tawny slung back with deliberate vulgarity, determined to tough out the confrontation so that he would never, ever suspect how much he had hurt her.

Navarre could barely conceal his distaste.

'You still owe me proof that that camera that recorded my supposed theft of your laptop has been wiped,' Tawny remarked less aggressively as that recollection returned to haunt her.

His sardonic mouth curled. 'There was no camera, no recording. That was a little white lie voiced to guarantee your good behaviour.'

'You're such a ruthless bastard,' Tawny quipped shakily, fighting a red tide of rage at how easily she had been taken in. Why had she not insisted on seeing that recording the instant he'd mentioned it?

'It got you off the theft hook,' he reminded her without hesitation.

'And you'll never forget that, will you?' But it wasn't really a question because she already knew the answer. She would *always* be a thief in Navarre Cazier's eyes and a woman he could buy for a certain price.

'Will you change your mind about the kiss-and-tell?'

Navarre asked harshly, willing her to surrender to his demand.

'Sorry, no…I want my five minutes of fame. Why shouldn't I have it? Have a safe journey home,' Tawny urged breezily.

'*Tu a un bon coup*…you're a good lay,' he breathed with cutting cool, and seconds later the door mercifully shut on his departure.

There was no hiding from the obvious fact that making love with him again had been a serious mistake and she mentally beat herself up for that misjudgement to such an extent that she did not sleep a wink for what remained of the night. Around seven in the morning she heard Jacques arrive to collect his employer's cases and later the sound of Navarre leaving the suite. Only when she was sure that he was gone did she finally emerge, pale and with shadowed eyes, from her room. She was shocked to find a bank draft for the sum of money he had agreed to pay her waiting on the table alongside her mobile phone. Was he making the point that, unlike her, once he had given his word he stuck to his agreements? He had ordered breakfast for eight o'clock as well and it arrived, the full works just as she liked, but the lump in her throat and the nausea in her tummy prevented her from eating anything. In the end she tucked the bank draft into her bag. Well, she couldn't just leave it lying there, could she? In the same way she packed the clothes he had bought her into the designer luggage and departed, acknowledging that in the space of a week he had turned her inside out.

CHAPTER EIGHT

'IF Tawny doesn't tell Cazier soon, I intend to do it for her,' Sergios Demonides decreed, watching his sister-in-law, Tawny, play ball in the sunshine with his older children, Paris, Milo and Eleni. Tawny's naturally slender figure made the swelling of her pregnant stomach blatantly obvious in a swimsuit.

'We can't interfere like that,' his wife, Bee, told him vehemently. 'He hurt her. She needs time to adapt to this new development—'

'How much time? Is she planning to wait until the baby is born and then tell him that he's a father?' Sergios reasoned, unimpressed. 'A man has a right to know that he has a child coming *before* its birth. Surely he cannot be as irresponsible as she is—'

'She's not irresponsible!' Bee argued, lifting their daughter, Angeli, into her arms as the black-haired toddler clasped her mother's knees to steady her still-clumsy toddler steps. 'She's just very independent. Have you any idea of how much persuasion I had to use to get her out here for a holiday?'

Outside Tawny glanced uneasily indoors to where her sister and her brother-in-law stood talking intently. She could tell that their attention was centred on her again and she flushed, wishing that Sergios would mind his own business and stop making her feel like such a nuisance. It was typical of the strong-willed Greek to regard his unmarried sister-in-law's pregnancy as a problem that was his duty to solve.

But that was the only cloud on her horizon in the wake of the wonderful week of luxurious relaxation she had enjoyed on Sergios's private island, Orestos. London had been cold and wintry when she flew out and she was returning there the following day, flying back to bad weather and her very ordinary job as a waitress in a restaurant. She felt well rested and more grounded after the break she had had with her sister and her lively family though. Sergios had become the guardian of his cousin's three orphaned children and with the recent addition of their own first child to the mix—the adorable Angeli—Bee was a very busy wife and mother. She was also very happy with her life, although that was an admission that went against the grain for Tawny, who was convinced that she could never have remained as even tempered and easy going as Bee in the radius of Sergios's domineering nature. Sergios was one of those men who knew the right way to do everything and it was always *his* way. And yet Bee had this magical knack of just looking at him sometimes when he was in full extrovert flood and he would suddenly shut up and smile at her as if she had waved a magic wand across his forbidding countenance.

'I can't bear to think of you going back to work such long hours. You should have rested more while you were here.' Bee sighed after dinner that evening as the two women sat out on the terrace watching the sun go down

'The way you did?' Tawny teased, recalling how incredibly hectic her half-sister's schedule had been while she was carrying her first child.

'I had Sergios for support…and my mother,' Bee reminded her.

Bee's disabled mother, Emilia, lived in a cottage in the grounds of their Greek home and was very much a member of their family. In comparison, Tawny's mother was living with her divorced boyfriend and his children in the house she had purchased with her inheritance from Tawny's grandfather. She was aghast that her daughter had fallen pregnant outside a relationship and had urged her to have a termination, an attitude that had driven yet another wedge into the already troubled relationship between mother and daughter. No, Tawny could not look for support from that quarter, and while her grandmother, Celestine, was considerably more tolerant when it came to babies, the older woman lived quite a long way from her and with the hours Tawny had to work she only saw the little Frenchwoman about once a month.

'It's a shame that you told Navarre that you *weren't* pregnant when he phoned you a couple of months ago,' Bee said awkwardly.

'I honestly thought it was the truth when I told him that. That first test I did *was* negative!' Tawny reminded the brunette ruefully. 'Do you really think I should have phoned him three weeks later and told him I'd been mistaken?'

'Yes.' Bee stayed firm in the face of the younger woman's look of reproach. 'It's Navarre's baby too. You have to deal with it. The longer you try to ignore the situation, the more complicated it will become.'

Tawny's eyes stung and she blinked furiously, turning her face away to conceal the turbulent emotions that seemed so much closer to the surface since she had fallen pregnant. She was fourteen weeks along now and she was changing shape rapidly with her tummy protruding, her

waist thickening and her breasts almost doubling in siz
Ever since she had learned that she had conceived she ha
felt horribly vulnerable and out of control of her body an
her life. All too well did she remember her mother's di
tressing tales of how Tawny's father had humiliated he
with his angry scornful attitude to her conception of
child he didn't want. Tawny had cringed at the prospe
of putting herself in the same position with a man wl
was already suspicious of her motives.

'I know that Navarre hurt you,' her half-sister mu
mured unhappily. 'But you should still tell him.'

'Somehow I fell for him like a ton of bricks,' Tawr
admitted abruptly, her voice shaking because it was t'
very first time she had openly acknowledged that unhap
truth, and Bee immediately covered her hand with hers
a gesture of quiet understanding. 'I never thought I cou
feel like that about a man and he was back out of my li
again before I even realised how much he had got to n
But there was nothing I could do to make things bett
between us—'

'How about just keeping your temper and talking
him?' Bee suggested. 'That would be a good place to ma
a start.'

Tawny didn't trust herself to do that either. How cou
she talk to a man who would almost certainly want l
to go for a termination? Why should she have to just'
her desire to bring her baby into the world just becaus
didn't suit him? So, she decided to text him the news la
that night, saving them both from the awkwardness o
direct confrontation when it was all too likely that eit
or both of them might say the wrong things.

*The first test I did was wrong. I am now 14 wee
pregnant,'* she informed him and added, utilising blc
capitals lest he cherish any doubts, *'It is YOURS.'*

Pressing the send button before she could lose her nerve, she slept that night soothed by the conviction that she had finally bitten the bullet and done what she had to do. Bee was shocked that her sister had decided to break the news in a text but Sergios believed that even that was preferable to keeping her condition a secret.

Navarre was already at work in his imposing office in Paris when Tawny's text came through and shock and disbelief roared through him like a hurricane-force storm. He wanted to disorder his immaculate cropped hair and shout to the heavens to release the steam building inside him as he read that text. *Merde alors!* She would be the death of him. How could she make such an announcement by text? How could she text 'YOURS' like that as if he were likely to argue the fact when she had been a virgin? He tried to phone her immediately but could not get an answer, for by then Tawny was already on board a flight to London. Within an hour Navarre had cancelled his appointments and organised a trip there as well.

Tawny stopped off at her bedsit only long enough to change for her evening shift at the restaurant and drop off her case. As she had decided that only actual starvation would persuade her to accept money from a man who had called her a good lay to her face, she had not cashed Navarre's bank draft and had had to work extremely hard to keep on top of all her financial obligations. Luckily some weeks back she had had the good fortune to sell a set of greeting card designs, which had ensured that Celestine's rent was covered for the immediate future. Tawny's work as a waitress paid her own expenses and, as her agent had been enthusiastic enough to send a selection of her Frenchman cartoons to several publications, she was even moderately hopeful that her cartoons might soon give her the break she had long dreamt of achieving.

Navarre seated himself in a distant corner of the self-service restaurant where Tawny worked and nursed a cup of the most disgusting black coffee he had ever tasted. Consumed by frustration over the situation she had created by keeping him out of the loop for so long, he watched her emerge from behind the counter to clear tables. And that fast his anger rose. Her streaming torrent of hair was tied back at the nape of her neck, her slender coltish figure lithe in an overall and leggings. At first glance she looked thinner but otherwise unchanged, he decided, subjecting her to a close scrutiny and noting the fined-down line of her jaw. Only when she straightened did he see the rounded swell of her stomach briefly moulded by the fabric of her tunic.

She was expecting his baby and even though she clearly needed to engage in hard menial work to survive, he reflected with brooding resentment and disapproval, she had still not made use of that bank draft he had left in the hotel for her. He had told his bank to inform him the instant the money was drawn and the weeks had passed and he had waited and waited, much as he had waited in vain for some sleazy kiss-and-tell about their affair to be published somewhere. When nothing happened, when his lowest expectations went totally unfulfilled, it had finally dawned on him that this was payback time Tawny-style. In refusing to accept that money from him, in disdaining selling 'their' story as she had threatened to do, she was taking her revenge, making her point that he had got her wrong and that she didn't need him for anything. Navarre understood blunt messages of a challenging nature, although she was the very first woman in his life to try and communicate with him on that aggressive level.

In addition, he had really not needed a shock phone call from her bossy sister Bee to tell him how *not* to handle her fiery half-sister. Bee Demonides had phoned him out of the blue just after his private jet landed in London and had introduced herself with aplomb. Tawny, he now appreciated, had kept secrets that he had never dreamt might exist in her background, secrets that sadly might have helped him to understand her better. Her sibling was married to one of the richest men in the world and Tawny had not breathed a word of that fact, had indeed 'oohed' and 'ahhed' over Sam Coulter's rented castle and the Golden Awards party as if she had no comparable connections or experiences. In fact, from what he had since established from Jacques's more wide-reaching enquiries, Tawny's other half-sister, Zara, was married to an Italian banker, who was also pretty wealthy. So, how likely was it that Tawny had ever planned to enrich herself by stealing Navarre's laptop to sell his secrets to the gutter press? On the other hand why did she feel the need to work in such lowly jobs when she had rich relatives who would surely have been willing to help her find more suitable employment? That was a complete mystery and only the first of several concerning Tawny Baxter, Navarre acknowledged impatiently.

Tawny was unloading a tray into a dishwasher in the kitchen when her boss approached her. 'There's a man waiting over by the far window for you…says he's a friend and he's here to tell you about a family crisis. I said that you could leave early—we're quiet this evening. I hope it's nothing serious.'

Tawny's first thought was that something awful had happened to her mother and that her mother's boyfriend, Rob, had come to tell her. Fear clenching her stomach, she grabbed her coat and bag and hurried back out into the restaurant, only to come to a shaken halt when she looked across the tables and saw Navarre seated in the far corner. His dark hair gleamed blue-black below the down lights that accentuated the stunning angles and hollows of his darkly handsome features. He threw back his head and she collided with brilliant bottle-green eyes and somehow she was moving towards him without ever recalling how she had reached that decision.

'Let's get out of here,' Navarre urged, striding forwards to greet her before she even got halfway to his table.

Still reeling in consternation from his sudden appearance, Tawny let him guide her outside and into the limousine pulling up at the kerb to collect them. Her hand trembled in the sudden firm hold of his, for their three months apart had felt like a lifetime and she could have done with advance warning of his visit. Thrown into his presence again without the opportunity to dress for the occasion and form a defensive shell, she felt horribly naked and unprepared. Once again, though, he had surprised her in a uniform that underlined the yawning gulf in their status.

'I wasn't expecting you—'

'You thought you could chuck a text bombshell at me and I was so thick-skinned that I would simply carry on as normal?' Navarre questioned with sardonic emphasis. 'Even I am not that insensitive.'

Tawny reddened. 'You took me by surprise.'

'Just as your text took me, *ma petite*.'

'Not so *petite* any longer,' she quipped.

'I noticed,' Navarre admitted flatly, his attention dropping briefly to the tummy clearly visible when she was sitting down. 'I'm still in shock.'

'Even after three months I'm still in shock.'

'Why did you tell me you weren't pregnant?'

'I did a test and it was negative. I think I did it too early. A few weeks later when I wasn't feeling well I bought another test and that one was positive. I didn't know how to tell you that I'd got it wrong—'

'*Exactement!* So, instead you took the easy way out and told me nothing.'

His sarcasm cut like the sudden slash of a knife against tender skin. 'Well, actually there was nothing easy about anything I've gone through since then, Navarre!' Tawny fired back at him in a sudden surge of spitfire temper. 'I've had all the worry without having anyone to turn to! I've had to work even though I was feeling as sick as a dog most mornings and the smell of cooking food made me worse, so working in a restaurant was not a pleasant experience. My hormones were all over the place and I've never felt so horribly tired in my life as I did those first weeks!'

'If only you had accepted the bank draft I gave you. We had an agreement and you earned that money by pretending to be my fiancée,' he reminded her grittily. 'But I understand why you refused to touch it.'

Her glacier blue eyes widened in disconcertion. 'You... do?'

'That last night we were together I was offensive, inexcusably so,' Navarre framed in a taut undertone, every word roughened by the effort it demanded of his pride to acknowledge such a fault to a woman.

That unexpected admission made it easier for Tawny to unbend in her turn. 'I made things worse. I shouldn't have pretended that I was planning to sell a story about you.'

'I made an incorrect assumption...time has proven me wrong, for no story appeared in the papers.'

'That note was smuggled in to me before we flew up to

Scotland. Julie would've been behind it. She even phoned my gran to try and find out where you and I had gone. I put the note in my pocket and forgot about it. I never intended to use that phone number.'

'Let the matter rest there. We have more important concerns at the moment.'

'How on earth did you find out where I was working?'

'You can thank your sister Bee for that information.'

Her exclamation of surprise was met by his description of the phone call he had received at the airport. Tawny winced and squirmed, loving Bee but deeply embarrassed by her interference. 'Bee hates people being at odds with each other. She's a tremendous peace maker but I do wish she had trusted me to handle this on my own.'

'She meant well. You're lucky to have a sister who cares so much about your welfare.'

'Zara is less pushy but equally opinionated.' At that point Tawny recalled Navarre telling her that he had no family he acknowledged and that memory filled her heart with regret and sympathy on his behalf. She might sometimes disagree with her relatives' opinions but she was still glad to have them in her life. People willing to tell her the truth and look out for her no matter what were a precious gift.

'Where are we heading?'

'Your sister and brother-in-law have kindly offered us the use of their home here in London for our meeting. We need somewhere to talk in private and I am tired of hotels,' he admitted curtly. 'It's time that I bought a property in this city.'

Tawny was pleased that Bee had offered the use of her luxury home in Chelsea and relieved not to have to take him back to her dreary bedsit to chat. Navarre, with his classy custom-made suits and shoes would never rela

LYNNE GRAHAM

against such a grungy backdrop and she did want him to relax. If they were going to share a child it was vitally important that they establish a more harmonious relationship, she reasoned ruefully.

Ushered into the elegant drawing room of Bee and Sergios's mansion home by their welcoming housekeeper, Tawny was grateful to just kick off her shoes and curl up on a well-upholstered sofa in comfort. All of a sudden she didn't care any more that she was looking less than her best in a work tunic with a touch of mascara being her only concession to cosmetic enhancement. After all, what did such things matter now? He was no longer interested in her in that way. Three months had passed since he had walked away from her without a backwards glance—she didn't count that single brief phone call made out of duty to ask if she was pregnant—and for such diametrically opposed personalities as they it had probably been a wise move.

Navarre marvelled at the manner in which she instantly shed all formality and made herself comfortable. She made no attempt to pose or impress him, had not even dashed a lipstick across her lush full mouth. He was used to women who employed a great deal more artifice and her casual approach intrigued him. In any case the lipstick would only have come off, he thought hungrily, appreciation snaking through him as he noted the purity of her fine-boned profile, the natural elegance of her slender body in relaxation. And that hint of a bump that had changed her shape was *his* child. It struck Navarre as quite bizarre at that moment that that thought should turn him on hard and fast.

Tawny was now thinking hard about their predicament, trying to be fair to both of them. Their baby was a complication of an affair that was already over and done with, she conceded unhappily, and the more honest she was with him now, the more likely they were to reach an agreement that suited both of them.

'I want to have this baby,' she told Navarre straight off, keen to avoid any exchange with him in regard to the choices she might choose to make for their child. 'My mother thinks I'm being an idiot because she believes that giving birth to me and becoming a single parent ruined her life. I've heard all the arguments on that score since I was old enough to understand what she was talking about but I don't feel the same way. This baby may not be planned but I love it already and we'll manage.'

'I like your positive attitude.'

'Do you?' She was warmed by the comment and a tremulous smile softened the stressful line of her pink mouth.

'But it does seem that we are both approaching this situation with a lot of baggage from our own childhoods.' Navarre compressed his hard sensual mouth as he voiced that comment. 'Neither of us had a father and we suffered from that lack. It is hard for a child to have only one parent.'

'Yes,' she agreed ruefully.

'And it also puts a huge burden on the single parent's shoulders. Your mother struggled to cope and became bitter while my mother could not cope with parenting me at all. Our experiences have taught us how hard it is to raise a child alone and I don't want to stand back and watch you and our child go through that same process.'

The extent of his understanding of the problems she might have took Tawny aback at the same time as his thoughtfulness and willingness to take responsibility impressed her. 'I'm not belittling my mother's efforts as a parent because she did the very best she could, but she was very bitter and I do think I'm more practical in my expectations than she was.'

'I don't think you should have to lower your expectations at your age simply because you will have a child's needs to consider.'

Tawny pulled a wry face. 'But we have to be realistic.'

'It is exactly because I am realistic about what life would be like for you that I've come here to ask you to marry me. Only marriage would allow me to take my full share of the responsibility,' Navarre told her levelly, his strong jawline squaring with resolve. 'Together we will be able to offer our child much more than we could offer as parents living apart.'

Tawny was totally stunned for she had not seen that option hovering on her horizon at all. She stared back at Navarre, noting how grave his face was, grasping by his composed demeanour that he had given the matter a great deal of thought. 'You're not joking, are you?'

'I want to be there for you from the moment this child is born,' Navarre admitted with tough conviction. 'I don't want another man to take my place in my child's life either. The best way forwards for both of us is marriage.'

'But we know so little about each other—'

'Is that important? Is it likely to make our relationship more successful? I think not,' he declared with assurance. 'I believe it is infinitely more important that we are strongly attracted to each other and both willing to make a firm commitment to raise our child together.'

Tawny was mesmerised by his rock solid conviction. She felt slightly guilty that she had not appreciated that he might feel as responsible for her well-being and for that of their child as he evidently did. Too late did she grasp that she had expected him to treat her exactly as her absent father had treated her mother—with disdain and resentment. He was not running away from the burden of childcare, he was moving closer to accept it. Tears of relief stung her eyes and she blinked rapidly, turning her face away in the hope he had not noticed.

But Navarre was too observant to be fooled. 'What's wrong, *chérie*? What did I say?'

Tawny smiled through the tears. 'It's all right, it's not you. It's just I cry over the silliest things at the minute—I think it's the hormones doing it. My father was absolutely horrible to my mum when she told him she was pregnant and I think I sort of subconsciously assumed you would be the same. So, you see, we're both guilty of making wrong assumptions.'

Navarre had tried to move on from his cynical suspicions about her, she reasoned with a feeling of warmth inside her that felt remarkably like hope. She had not cashed the bank draft, she had not talked to the press about him and as a result he was willing to reward her with his trust. He treated her now with respect. He was no longer questioning the manner of their baby's conception or even mentioning a cynical need for DNA testing to check paternity. In short he had cut through all the rubbish that had once littered their relationship and offered her a wedding ring as a pledge of commitment to a new future. And she knew immediately that she would say yes to his proposal, indeed that it would feel like a sin not to at least try to see if they could make a marriage work for the sake of their child.

This was the guy whom against all the odds she had fallen madly in love with. He was the guy who ordered her magnificent breakfasts and admired her appetite and constantly checked that she wasn't hungry, the guy who had batted not a single magnificent eyelash over those embarrassing newspaper revelations about her background in spite of the presence of a bunch of snobbish socialite guests, who had undoubtedly looked down on his bargain basement taste in fiancées. He was also the guy who was endearingly, ridiculously jealous and possessive if another man so much as looked at her, an attitude which had made her feel irresistible for the first time in her life.

'Do you like children?' she asked him abruptly.

Navarre laughed. 'I've never really thought about it, but, yes, I believe that I do.'

When he smiled like that the power of his charisma rocketed, throwing him into the totally gorgeous bracket, and he made her heart hammer and her breath catch in her throat. 'Yes, I'll marry you,' she told him in French.

'You're an artist. I believe you will like living in Paris.'

He made it all seem so simple. That first visit he insisted on meeting her mother and her partner over dinner the following night at a very smart hotel. At first mother and daughter were a little stiff with each other, but at the end of the evening Susan Baxter took Tawny to one side to speak to her in private and said, 'I'm so happy it's all working out for you that I don't really know what to say,' she confided, tears shining in her anxious gaze. 'I know you were annoyed with the solution I suggested but I just didn't want your life to go wrong while you were still so young. I was afraid that you were repeating my mistakes and it felt like that had to be my fault—'

'Navarre's not like my father,' Tawny cut in with perceptible pride.

'No, he seems to be very mature and responsible.'

The word 'responsible' stung, although Tawny knew that no insult had been intended. She was too sensitive, she acknowledged ruefully. Navarre would not walk away from his child because he had grown up without the support of either a father or a mother and only he knew what that handicap had cost him. For that reason he would not abandon the mother of his child to struggle with parenthood alone. Acknowledging that undeniable fact made Tawny feel just a little like a charity case or an exercise in which Navarre would prove to his own satisfaction that he had the commitment gene, which his own parents had sadly lacked. It was an impression that could have been dissolved overnight had Navarre made the smallest attempt to become intimate with his intended bride again... but he did not. The pink diamond was placed on her engagement finger again, for real this time around, but his detached attitude, his concentration on the practical rather than the personal, left Tawny feeling deeply insecure and vulnerable.

Bee and Sergios offered to stage Navarre and Tawny's wedding at their London home and under pressure from Tawny, after initially refusing that offer Navarre agreed to it. He then rented a serviced apartment for Tawny's use and at his request she immediately gave up her job as a waitress and moved into the apartment while he returned to Paris. From there he hired a property firm to find them an ideal home in London and she spent her time doing viewings of the kind of luxury property she had never dreamt she might one day call home.

Only days after Tawny told her other half-sister, Zara, that she was getting married, Zara arrived in London for an unexpected visit, having left her children, Donata and her infant son, Piero, at home with her husband outside Florence.

'Does this visit now mean you aren't able to come to the wedding next week?' Tawny asked, surprised by the timing of her sister's trip to London. 'I know it was short notice but—'

'No, I just wanted the chance to talk to you alone *before* the wedding,' Zara completed with rather tense emphasis.

Drawing back from her half-sibling's hug, Tawny frowned. 'What's up? Oh, my goodness, you and Vitale aren't having trouble, are you?' she prompted in dismay, for the other couple had always seemed blissfully happy together.

Her dainty blonde sister went pink with discomfiture. 'Oh, no…no, nothing like that!' she exclaimed, although her eyes remained evasive.

The two young women settled in the comfortable lounge with coffee and biscuits. Tawny looked at Zara expectantly. 'So, tell me…'

Zara grimaced. 'I truly didn't know whether to come and talk to you or not. Bee said I should mind my own business and keep my mouth shut, so I discussed it with Vitale, but he thought I should be more honest with you.'

Tawny was frowning. 'R-right…I'm sorry, I don't understand.'

'It's something about Navarre, just rumours, but they've been around a long time and I don't know whether you know about them or even *should* know about them.' Her tongue tying her into increasingly tight knots, Zara was openly uncomfortable. 'I wouldn't usually repeat gossip—'

Tawny's spine went rigid with tension. Zara was a gentle kind person, never bitchy or mean. If Zara felt there were rumours about Navarre that Tawny ought to hear, she reckoned that they would very probably be a genuine source of concern for her. 'I'd like to say that I don't listen to gossip, but I'm not sure I could live without knowing now that you've told me there's something you think I should know about my future husband.'

'Now remember that I'm married to an Italian,' Zara reminded her uneasily. 'And for many years in Italy there have been strong rumours to the effect that Navarre Cazier is engaged in a long-running secret affair with Tia Castelli…you know the Italian movie star…?'

CHAPTER NINE

TAWNY who had literally stopped breathing while Zara spoke, relocated her lungs at the sound of that name and started to breathe again.

'My goodness, is there anyone on this planet who hasn't heard of Tia Castelli?' Tawny asked with her easy laugh. 'Are there rumours about Navarre and Tia having an affair? *Truthfully?* When I saw them together—'

Zara leant forwards in astonishment. 'You've already met Tia Castelli? You've actually seen her with Navarre? The word is that they're in constant contact.'

Tawny told her sister about her appearance by Navarre's side at the Golden Awards and her encounter with Tia and her husband, Luke.

'Surprising,' Zara remarked thoughtfully. 'I should think if that there had been anything sneaky going on Navarre would have avoided their company like the plague.'

'Navarre has known Tia for years and years. He worked for the banker that handled Tia's investments—that's how they first met,' Tawny explained frankly. 'Tia is very flirtatious. She expects to be the centre of attention but she's perfectly pleasant otherwise. I think you'd best describe her as being very much a man's woman.'

'So, you didn't notice anything strange between her

and Navarre? Anything that made you uncomfortable?'
Zara checked.

All Tawny felt uncomfortable about at that moment was
that she did not feel she could tell Zara the truth of how
she had met Navarre and become his fiancée, because she
and Navarre had already agreed that now their relationship
had become official nobody else had any need to know
about their previous arrangement. But it did occur to her
just then that the night she had met Tia Castelli, she had
been no more than a hired companion on Navarre's terms
and he had had less reason to hide anything from her. He
had been very attentive towards Tia, almost protective,
she recalled, struggling to think back and recapture what
she had seen. And Tia *was* an extraordinarily beautiful
and appealing woman. Tawny wondered if she was being
ridiculously naive about their relationship and could not
help recalling Luke Convery's annoyance at his wife's
friendship with Navarre. No smoke without fire, she reasoned ruefully. It was perfectly possible that Navarre and
Tia *had* been lovers at some point in the past.

'Now I've got you all worked up and worried! I
should've kept quiet! Why is Bee always right?' Zara exclaimed guiltily as she tracked the fast changing expres-
sions on the younger woman's face. 'She would never ever
have mentioned those stupid rumours to you.'

Ironically, what Tawny was thinking about then was
the number of times she had heard Navarre talking on
the phone in Italian, a language that he seemed to speak
with the fluency of a native. Could he have been speaking to Tia? Surely not every time she had heard him using
Italian, though, she told herself irritably, for that would
have meant that he talked to the gorgeous blonde almost
every day.

At the end of the afternoon, when Zara departed as-

suring Tawny that she and her husband would attend her
wedding, Tawny was conscious that there was now a tiny
little seed of doubt planted inside her that was more than
ready to sprout into a sturdy sapling of suspicion.

Prior to her pregnancy, Navarre had seemed so hungry for Tawny, but not so hungry that he had made any
attempt to get her back into bed in advance of the wedding. Who had been satisfying that hot libido of his during the three months of their separation? And why was
she thinking that him having wanted her automatically
meant he could not have also wanted Tia Castelli? Was
she really that unsophisticated? After all, Tia was married and the sort of catch many men would kill to possess
even briefly. Even if Tia and Navarre were having an affair Tia must surely accept that there would also be other
women in Navarre's life. Her peace of mind shattered by
that depressing conclusion, Tawny went to bed to toss and
turn, troubled by her thoughts but determined not to share
what she still deemed might be ridiculous suspicions with
Navarre. Revealing such concerns when she had no proof
would make her look foolish and put her at a disadvantage.

In the middle of the night she got up and performed
an Internet search of Tia and Navarre's names together to
discover any links that there might be. An hour later she
had still not got to the end of the references, but had discovered nothing definitive, nothing that could not be explained by honest friendship. There were several pictures
of Tia and Navarre chatting in public places, not a single
one of anything more revealing—no holding of hands, no
embraces, *nothing*. And if the paparazzi had failed to establish a more intimate link, the likelihood was that there
wasn't one, for Tia Castelli's every move was recorded by
the paps. But ironically for the first time Tawny was now
wondering what had been on Navarre's laptop that he had

so feared having exposed. What had Julie's high-paying journalist really hoped to find out from that computer? About the buyout of CCC? Her worst fears assuaged by that idea, for she recalled Navarre's comment about the deal already being in the news, Tawny went back to bed.

It was a wonderful wedding dress, fashioned by a designer to conceal the growing evidence of the bride's pregnancy. Tawny looked at her reflection in the mirror with her sisters standing anxiously by her side and then hugged Zara, who had located the glorious dress, which bared her shoulders and her newly impressive chest in a style that removed attention from her abdomen.

'You've sure got boobs now, babe,' Zara pronounced with a giggle.

Tawny grinned, her lovely face lighting up for it was true: for the first time ever she had the bosom bounty that she had always lacked and no padding was required.

'Are you happy?' Bee prompted worriedly. 'You're sure Navarre is the right man for you?'

Tawny lifted a hand to brush a wondering finger across the magnificent diamond tiara that anchored her veil and added height to her slim figure. 'Well, it's either him or the diamonds he's just given me,' she teased. 'But it all feels incredibly right.'

An offer had been made and accepted on a town house with a garden in the same area in which Bee and Sergios lived. In a few weeks' time it would provide a very comfortable base for her and Navarre when they were in London, ensuring that she need never feel that she was being taken away from absolutely everything she had ever known. She was on a high because everything in her world seemed to be blossoming. After all, she had just sold her first cartoons as well. One of the publications that her agent had sent her work to had shared them with a French sister magazine and the French editor had offered Tawny a contract to create more of her Frenchman drawings. Ecstatic at the news, Tawny had still to share it with Navarre because she wanted to surprise him by putting the magazine in front of him when the first cartoon appeared in print.

'You should've let me twist Dad's arm to give you away,' Zara lamented. 'He would have done it if I'd pushed him.'

'I don't know our father, Zara. I wouldn't have wanted him to do it just to please you and Bee. I much prefer Sergios. At least he genuinely wishes Navarre and I well,' Tawny pointed out.

Her opinion of Sergios had recently warmed up, for it was thanks to Sergios and his managing ways that her grandmother, Celestine, was being whisked to London in a limousine for the wedding and put up that night in Bee's home so that the extended celebration was not too much of a strain for the old lady.

At the church, Tawny breathed in deep, her hand resting lightly on Sergios's arm before she moved down the aisle, her sisters following her clad in black and cream outfits. All her attention locked to Navarre, who had flown back to France within days of his proposal, she moved slowly towards the altar. Devastatingly handsome in a tailored silver-grey suit teamed with a smart waistcoat and cravat, Navarre took her breath away just as he had the very first time she saw him and she hugged the knowledge to herself that he would soon be her husband. As she reached the altar Celestine, a tiny lady with a mop of white curls, turned her head to beam at her granddaughter.

Although Tawny's head told her that she was entering a shotgun marriage of the utmost practicality, it didn't feel like one. She loved the ceremony, the sure way Navarre made his responses, the firm hold of the hand on hers as he slid on the wedding ring. In her heart she felt that he was making a proper commitment to her and their child. Before they left the church Navarre took the time to stop and greet her grandmother, whom he had not had time to meet beforehand.

'Do you like the dress?' she asked him once they were alone in the limo conveying them back to her sister's home.

'I like what's in it even better, *ma petite,*' Navarre confided, his attention ensnared by the luminosity of her beautiful eyes, and momentarily a pang of regret touched him for the parts of his life that he could never share with her. He had always believed that as long as he kept his life simple nothing could go wrong, but from the instant Tawny had walked into his life to try to steal his laptop his every plan had gone awry and things had stopped happening the way he had assumed they would. He didn't like that, he had learned to prefer the predictable and the safe, but he told himself that now that they were married his daily life would return to its normal routine. Why should anything have to change?

Tawny gazed dizzily into beautiful emerald-green eyes framed by black spiky lashes and her heart hammered. Her breasts swelled beneath her bodice, the pointed tips straining into sudden tingling life. His attention was on her mouth. The tip of her tongue slid out to moisten her lower lip and he tensed, his sleek strong face hard and taut. The silence lay heavy, thick like the sensual spell flooding her treacherous body, and she leant closer, propelled by promptings much stronger than she was.

'I'll wreck your make-up,' Navarre growled, but a hard hand closed into the back of her veil to hold her still while his mouth plundered hers with fierce heat and hunger, the delving of his tongue sending every skin cell she possessed mad with excitement.

Tawny wanted to push him flat on the back seat and have her wicked way with him. That fast her body was aching with need and ready for him. Her fingers flexed on a long powerful masculine thigh and then slid upwards to establish that the response was not one-sided. He was hard and thick and as eager as she was and even as he pushed back from her, surprise at her boldness etched in his intent gaze, she was content to have discovered that the exact same desire powered them both. Her face was flushed as she eased away from him, her body quivering with the will power it took to do so.

'*Mon Dieu, ma belle*...you make me ache like a boy again,' he confessed raggedly.

And the gloss on Tawny's day was complete. Happy at the response she had received, reassured by his desire, she sailed into her wedding reception in the ballroom of her sister's magnificent home. Perhaps he had only restrained himself sexually with her out of some outmoded idea of respecting her as his future wife, she thought buoyantly, for she had noticed that Navarre could sometimes be a shade old-fashioned in his outlook. Whatever, her insecurity was gone, her awareness of her pregnancy as a source of embarrassment banished while she held her head high and stood by his side to welcome the wealthy powerful guests whom Navarre counted as friends and business connections. Only recently she would only have got close to such people by waiting on them in some menial capacity, but now she met with them as an equal. Tia Castelli kissed her cheek with cool courtesy, her previous warmth muted, while her husband, Luke, gave Tawny a lazy smile. Tawny perfectly understood and forgave Tia for that dash of coolness in her manner, for the actress had to be aware that a married man would be far less available to her than a single guy.

Later that afternoon, it did her heart good when Bee drew her attention to the fact that Navarre was sitting with her grandmother, Celestine. 'They've been talking for ages,' her half-sister informed her.

Tawny drifted over to Navarre's side and he laced long fingers with hers to tug her down into a seat beside him. 'You've been holding out on me, *chérie*.'

'And me,' Celestine added. 'All these months I had no idea you were paying my rent.'

Tawny froze. 'What on earth are you talking about?'

'One of the other residents spoke to me about his problems meeting the maintenance costs and when certain sums were mentioned I knew that I did not have enough money to meet such enormous bills either,' the old lady told her quietly. 'I spoke to my solicitor and although he didn't break your confidence, I soon worked out for myself that there was only one way that my costs could be being met. I felt very guilty for not realising what was going on sooner.'

'Don't be daft, Gran…I've managed fine!' Tawny protested, upset that the older woman had finally registered the level to which her expenses had exceeded her means.

'By slaving away as a chambermaid and waiting on tables,' Celestine responded unhappily. 'That was not right and I would never have agreed to it.'

'I've reassured Celestine that as a member of the family I will be taking care of any problems from now on and that I hope she will be a regular visitor to our home.'

Tawny sat down beside him to soothe the old lady's worries and with Navarre's support Celestine's distress gradually faded away. Soon after that her grandmother admitted that she was tired and Tawny saw her up to the room she was to use until her departure the next morning.

'Navarre is...*très sympathique*,' her grandmother pronounced with approval. 'He is kind and understanding. You will be very happy with him.'

Having helped her grandmother unpack her overnight bag and locate all the facilities, Tawny hurried back downstairs to find Navarre waiting for her at the foot. 'Why didn't you tell me what you needed the money for months ago?' he demanded in a driven undertone, his incredulity at her silence on that score unhidden.

'It was nothing to do with you. She's my granny.'

'And now she's mine as well and you will change no more beds on her behalf!' Navarre asserted fierily.

'It's not a problem. I never had a burning desire to be a maid but it was easy work to find and it allowed me to do my illustration projects in the evenings.'

He tilted up her chin. His gaze was stern. 'Couldn't you have trusted me enough to tell me the truth for yourself?' he pressed. 'I assumed your loyalty could be bought—I thought less of you for being willing to take that money from me in payment.'

'Only because you've forgotten what it's like to be poor and in need of cash,' Tawny told him tartly. 'Poverty has no pride. When I was a child, my grandparents were very good to me. I'd do just about anything to keep Celestine safe, secure and happy.'

'And I honour you for it and for all your hard work for her benefit, *ma petite*. You also took on that responsibility without any expectation of ever receiving her gratitude, for you tried to hide your contributions to her income. I'm hugely impressed,' Navarre admitted, his stunning gaze warm with pride and approval on her blushing face. 'But why didn't you approach your sisters for help?'

'Celestine isn't related to them in any way. I wouldn't dream of bothering them for money,' Tawny argued in consternation.

'I suspect Bee would have liked to help—'

'Maybe so, Navarre,' his bride responded. 'But I've always believed in standing on my own two feet.'

An hour later when Tawny was chatting to her mother and her partner, Susan commented on how effective her daughter's dress was at concealing her swelling stomach. Amused, Tawny splayed her hand to her abdomen, momentarily moulding the fabric to the definite bulge of her pregnancy. 'My bump's still there beneath the fancy trappings!' she joked.

A few feet away, she glimpsed Tia Castelli staring at her fixedly, big blue eyes wide, her flawless face oddly frozen and expressionless before, just as quickly, the actress spun round and vanished into the crush of guests. As Tawny frowned in incomprehension Bee signalled her by pointing at her watch: it was time for Tawny to change out of her finery, and she followed her sibling upstairs because she and Navarre were leaving for France in little more than an hour. Twenty minutes later, Tawny descended a rear staircase a couple of steps in Bee's wake. She was wearing a very flattering blue skirt with floral silk tee and a long flirty jacket teamed with impossibly high heels.

Bee stopped dead so suddenly at the foot of the stairs that Tawny almost tripped over her. 'Let's go back up…I forgot something!' she exclaimed in a peculiar whisper.

But Tawny was not that easily distracted and Bee, unfortunately, was not a very good actress when she was surprised and upset by something. Correctly guessing that her sister had seen something she did not want her to see, Tawny ignored Bee's attempt to catch her arm and prevent her from stepping into the corridor at the bottom of the stairs. Tawny moved past and caught a good view of the scene that Bee had sought to protect her from. Tia Castelli was sobbing on Navarre's chest as if her heart were breaking and he was looking down at the tiny blonde with that highly revealing mixture of concern and tenderness that only existed in the most intimate of relationships. Certainly one look at the manner in which her bridegroom was comforting Tia was sufficient to freeze Tawny in her tracks and cut through her heart like a knife. It was a little vignette of her worst nightmares for, while she had from the outset accepted that Navarre did not love her, she had never been prepared for the reality that he might love another woman instead.

Abruptly registering that they had acquired an audience, Navarre stepped back and Tia flipped round to make a whirlwind recovery, eyes damp but enquiring, famous face merely anxious. 'I had a stupid row with Luke, I'm afraid, and Navarre swept me off to save me from making a fool of myself about it in public.'

It was a wry and deft explanation voiced as convincingly as only a skilled actress could make it. It sounded honest and it might even have been true, Tawny reckoned numbly, but she just didn't believe it. What she had seen was something more, something full of stronger, darker emotions on both sides. Tia's distress had been genuine even though it was hidden now, the blonde's perfect face tear-stained but composed in a light apologetic smile.

'I understand,' Tawny said flatly, for she had too much pride and common sense to challenge either of them when she had no evidence of wrongdoing. But in the space of a moment fleeting suspicion had turned into very real apprehension and insecurity.

'You look charming, *chèrie*,' Navarre murmured smoothly, scanning her shuttered face with astute cool.

He would give nothing away for free. No information, no secrets, no apologies. He would not put himself on the defensive. She knew that. She had married a master tactician, a guy to whom manipulation was a challenging game, which his intelligence and courage ensured he would always excel at playing.

Pale though she was, Tawny smiled as if she had not a worry in the world either. She hoped he would not notice that the smile didn't reach her eyes. She suspected that he was probably more relieved that she did not speak Italian and therefore was quite unable to translate the flood of words Tia had been sobbing at the moment they were disturbed. But at that instant Tawny also realised that someone had been present who could speak Tia's native tongue and she glanced at her linguistically talented sister Bee, who was noticeably pale as well, and resolved to question her as to what she had overheard before they parted.

When they returned to the ballroom, there was no sign of Tia or Luke and Tawny was not surprised by that strategic retreat. Promising Navarre she would be back within minutes, Tawny set off to find her sister again. She was even less surprised to find Bee talking to Zara, both their faces tense and troubled.

'OK…I'm the unlucky woman who just married a guy and caught a famous film star hanging round his neck like an albatross!' Tawny mocked. 'Bee, tell me what Tia was saying.'

Her sisters exchanged a conspiratorial glance.

'No, it's not fair to keep it from me. I have a right to know what you heard.'

Bee parted her lips with obvious reluctance. 'Tia was upset about the baby. I don't think she had realised that you were pregnant.'

'She was probably jealous. She's never been able to have a child of her own,' Zara commented.

'But the normal person to share that grief with would be her own husband, not *mine*,' Tawny completed with gentle emphasis. 'Don't worry about me. This isn't a love match. I've always known that. This marriage may not work out...not if that woman owns a slice of Navarre. I couldn't live with that, I couldn't *share* him—'

'I don't think that you have anything to worry about. Now if you'd caught them in a clinch that would've been a different matter,' Bee offered quietly. 'But you *didn't*. Don't let that colourful imagination of yours take over, Tawny. Be sensible about this. I think all you witnessed was a gorgeous drama queen demanding attention from a handsome man. I suspect that Tia is an old hand at that ruse and Navarre looked a little out of his depth. I also think that from now on he will be more careful with his boundaries when he's around Tia Castelli. He's no fool.'

Tawny struggled to take Bee's advice fully on board while she and Navarre were conveyed to the airport. He chatted calmly about their day and she endeavoured to make appropriate responses but she could not deny that the joy of the day had been snuffed out for her the instant she saw Navarre comforting Tia. She felt overwhelmed by the competition. What woman could possibly compete with such a fascinating femme fatale? Tia Castelli was a hugely talented international star with a colossal number of fans, an extraordinary beauty who truly lived a gilded life that belonged only in the glossiest of magazines. And Navarre *cared* about Tia. Tawny had seen the expression on his face as he looked down at the tiny distressed woman and that glimpse had shaken her and wounded her for she would have given ten years of her life to have her bridegroom look at her like that even once. That, she thought painfully, was what really lay at the heart of her suffering. Seeing him with Tia had only underlined what Tawny did not have with him.

But she would still have to man up and handle it, Tawny told herself in an urgent pep talk while they flew to Paris on Navarre's sleek private jet. She could not run away on the very first day of married life. She would only get one chance to make their marriage work so that they could give their son or daughter a proper loving home with a mother *and* a father. It was what she had always longed for and always lacked on her own account, but perhaps she had been naive as well not to face the truth that any relationship between two people would at times hurt her and demand that she compromise her ideals.

By the time they were in a limousine travelling to his home on Ile de France, several miles west of Paris, Navarre had borne the silence long enough. It was not a sulk—a sulk he could have dealt with. No, Tawny spoke when spoken to, even smiled when forced, but her vibrant spirit and quirky sense of fun were nowhere to be seen and it spooked him.

'I don't know you like this…what's wrong?' he asked, although it was a question that on principle he never, ever asked a woman, but now he was asking even though he feared that he already knew the answer.

Tawny shot him another fake smile. 'I'm just a bit tired, that's all. It's been a very long day.'

'*D'accord.* I constantly forget that you're pregnant and I'm making no allowances for that,' Navarre responded smoothly. 'Of course you're tired.'

It was on the tip of her tongue to tell him that it was their wedding night and she wasn't *that* tired but that would have been like issuing an invitation and she no longer possessed the confidence to do that.

The awkward silence was broken by her gasp as she looked out of the window and saw that the car was travelling through elaborate gardens and heading straight for a multi-turreted chateau of such stupendous splendour that she could only stare. 'Where on earth are we?'

'This is my home in Paris.'

'You're sure it's not a hotel?' Tawny asked stupidly, aghast at the size and magnificence of the property.

'It was for a while but it is now my private home. It's within easy reach of my offices and I like green space around me at the end of the day.'

Yes, it was obvious to her that he liked an enormous amount of green space and even more obvious why he had not been unduly impressed by Strathmore Castle, the entirety of which might well have fitted into the front hall of his spectacular chateau. Tawny was gobsmacked by the dimensions of the place. Although they had flown from London in a private jet it had still not occurred to her that Navarre might live like royalty in France. Nor had not it crossed her mind until that very moment what a simply vast gulf divided them as people.

'I feel like Cinderella,' Tawny whispered weakly. 'You live in a castle.'

He was frowning. 'I thought you'd be pleased.'

They were greeted by a manservant in the echoing vastness of the hall and every surface seemed to be gilded or marbled or mirrored so that she could see far too many confusing reflections of her bewildered face. 'It's not really a castle, it's more like a palace,' she muttered when he informed her that refreshments awaited them upstairs.

She mounted the giant staircase. 'So how long have you lived here?'

'Several years. You know, you shouldn't be wearing heels that high in your condition—'

'Navarre?' Tawny interrupted. 'Don't tell me what to wear. I'm not working for you any more.'

'No, we're married now.'

Tawny did not like the tone Navarre had employed to make that statement. She felt that he ought to be over the moon about being married to her, or at least capable of pretending to be. Instead he sounded like a guy who had got to bring the wrong woman home and that was not an idea that she liked at all, for it came all too close to matching her own worst fears.

'I don't want to have an argument with you on our wedding day,' Navarre informed her without any expression at all.

'Did I say that I wanted an argument?' Tawny demanded a touch stridently as he thrust open a heavy door and she stalked into yet another vast room, a bedroom complete with sofas and tables and several exit doors. 'It's too big…it's *all* too big and fancy for me!'

As her voice began to rise in volume Navarre cut in. 'Then we'll sell it and move—'

'But then you wouldn't be happy. This is what you're used to!'

'I grew up in a variety of slums,' he reminded her levelly and somehow the way he looked at her made her feel like a child throwing a tantrum.

Tawny gritted her teeth on another foolish comment. Her brain was all over the place. It certainly wasn't functioning as it should be. She kept on picturing Tia's flawless face and her even more perfect and always immaculately clothed body. She was thinking of the frivolous, frothy wedding night negligee she had purchased with such joy in her heart and feeling sick at the prospect of having to put the outfit on and appear in it for his benefit. Who was she kidding? It would not hide her overblown breasts or her even more swollen stomach.

'You know…' Tawny mumbled uneasily, succumbing to her sense of insecurity. 'I'm not really in the right mood for a wedding night.'

'Je sais ce que tu ressens…I know how you feel.' Navarre stood there like a statue.

Tawny had expected him to argue with her, not agree with her. She wanted him to kiss her, persuade her, make everything magically all right again, but instead he just stood there, six feet plus of inert and unresponsive masculine toughness.

'You're tired, *ma petite*. I'll sleep elsewhere.'

Tawny recognised the absolute control he was exerting not to let her see what he really thought. She suspected that he was annoyed with her, that he had hoped she would continue as though nothing whatsoever had happened, as though nothing at all had changed between them. But how could she do that? How *could* she pretend she had not seen the way he looked at Tia? He had never looked at her like that, but she so badly needed him to and, denied what she most wanted, she refused to settle for being a substitute for Tia. And, to be frank, a very poor second-best at that.

Wishing her goodnight with infuriating courtesy, Navarre left the room. Her legs weak, Tawny sagged down on the sofa at the end of the bed as though she had gone ten rounds with a champion boxer. He was gone and she was no happier. She was at the mercy of as many doubts as a fishing net had holes. Had she done the wrong thing? What was the right thing in such circumstances when all she was conscious of was the level of her disillusionment? She turned her bright head to look at the big bed that they might have shared that night had she been tougher and more practical and she imagined she heard the sound of a sharp painful crack—it was the sound of her heart breaking…

CHAPTER TEN

TAWNY signed the cartoon and sat back from it with a sense of accomplishment. She was working in the room that Navarre had had set up as a studio for her. For the first time in her creative life she had the latest in light tables to work at. Her cartoon series now entitled 'The English Wife' and carried in a fashionable weekly magazine, had already attracted a favourable wave of comment from the French press and she had even been interviewed in her capacity as cartoonist and wife of a powerful French industrialist. A knock on the door announced the arrival of Gaspard, who was in charge of the household and the staff, bringing her morning coffee and a snack.

On the surface life was wonderful, Tawny acknowledged, striving to concentrate only on the positive angles. Navarre had been in London the previous night on a business trip, but Tawny had not accompanied him because she had work to complete. Furthermore just as he had forecast she adored Paris: the noble architecture of the buildings, beautiful bridges and cobblestoned streets, the Seine gleaming below the autumn sunlight, the entertaining parade of chic residents. Settling in for someone who spoke French and was married to a Frenchman had not proved much of a challenge. In fact her new life in France was absolutely brilliant now that her career had finally taken off. She had no financial worries, a beautiful roof over her head covered with all the turrets a castle-loving girl could ever want and a staff who ensured that she had to do virtually nothing domestic for herself. The food was amazing as well, Tawny conceded, munching hungrily through the kind of dainty little pastry that Navarre's chef excelled at creating.

In fact after six weeks of being married to Navarre, Tawny was willing to admit that she was a very lucky woman. Cradling her coffee in one hand, Tawny studied herself in a wall mirror. Her hair piled on top of her head in a convenient style that her hairdresser had taught her to do, she was wearing her favourite skinny jeans teamed with an artfully draped jersey tunic that skimmed her growing bump and long suede boots. She had signed up with a Parisian obstetrician and her pregnancy was proceeding well. She had no problems on that front at all: she was ridiculously healthy.

Indeed her only problem was her marriage…or, to be more specific, the marriage that had never got off the ground in the first place. With the calmer frame of mind brought on by the passage of several weeks, she knew that wrecking their wedding night and rejecting Navarre had been the wrong thing to do. An outright argument would have been preferable; a demand for an explanation about that scene with Tia would have been understandable. But refusing to ask questions and hiding behind her wounded pride had not been a good idea at all, for it had imposed a distance between them that was impossible to eradicate in such a very large house. My goodness, he was sleeping two corridors away from her! And she had only found that out by tiptoeing round like a cat burglar in the dark of the night and listening to where he went when he came upstairs at the end of the evening.

There were times, many many times, when Tawny just
wanted to *scream* at Navarre in frustration. He did not
avoid her but he did work fairly long hours. At the same
time she could not accuse him of neglecting her either because he had gone to considerable lengths to make time
and space for her presence in his life and show her Paris
as only a native could. He would phone and arrange to
meet her for lunch or dinner or sweep her off shopping
with an alacrity that astonished her. Navarre was a very
woman-savvy male. When she was in his company he
awarded her his full attention and he was extraordinarily
charming, but he still continued to maintain a hands-off
approach that was driving her crazy.

Sometimes she wondered if Navarre was very clev-
erly and with great subtlety punishing her for that rejec-
tion on the first night. He took her romantic places and
left her as untouched as if she were his ninety-year-old
maiden aunt. He had introduced her to Ladurée, an opu-
lently designed French café/ gallery where the beautiful
people met early evening for coffee and delicious pastel-
coloured macaroons that melted in the mouth. He had
shown her the delights of La Hune, a trendy bookshop in
the bohemian sixth *arrondissement* of St-Germain. He
had taken her shopping on the famous designer rue St—
Honoré and spent a fortune on her. She had toured the
colourful organic market at boulevard Raspail and eaten
pumpkin muffins fresh from a basket. They had dined at
Laperouse, a dimly lit ornate restaurant beside the Seine,
an experience that had cried out for a more intimate connection and she had sat across the table willing him to
make a move on her or even voice a flirtatious comment,
only to be disappointed.

And then there were the gifts he brought her, featuring everything from an art book that had sent her into

ecstasies to a pair of Louboutin shoes that sparkled like pure gold, not to mention the most gorgeous jewels and flowers. He was never done buying her presents, indeed he rarely came home empty-handed. She had got the message: he was generous, he liked to *give*. But how was she supposed to respond? Her teeth gritted. She really didn't understand the guy she had married because she didn't know what he wanted from her. Was he content with their relationship as it was? A platonic front of a marriage for the sake of their child? Were the constant gifts and entertaining outings a reward for not questioning his relationship with Tia Castelli? Could he possibly be that callous and without scruples?

Yet this was the same man who had gripped her hand in genuine joy and appreciation when he attended a sonogram appointment with her and they saw their child together for the first time on a screen. The warmth of his response had been everything she could have hoped for. Their little girl, the daughter whom Tawny already cherished in her heart, would rejoice in a fully committed and ardent father. She knew enough about Navarre to understand how very important it was for him to do everything for his child that had not been done for him. He might hide his emotions, but she knew they ran deep and true when it came to their baby. It hurt not to inspire an atom of that emotion on her own account.

After a light lunch, she walked round the gardens until a light mist of drizzling rain came on and drove her indoors. She was presented with a package that had been delivered and she carried it upstairs, wondering ruefully what the latest treat was that Navarre had bought her. She extracted an elaborate box and, opening it, worked through layers of tissue paper to extract the most exquisite set of silk lingerie she had ever seen in her life. A dreamy smile

softened her full mouth and her pale eyes flared with the
thought of the possibilities awakened by that more intimate present. Her fingers dallied with the delicate set. An
invitation? Or was that wishful thinking? Was it just one
more in a long line of wonderfully special gifts? Maybe
she should wear it to meet him off his flight this evening
and just ask him what he meant by it. That outrageous
thought made her laugh out loud.

But that same thought worked on her throughout the
afternoon. Maybe a little plain speaking was all that was
required to sort out their marriage. And Navarre was far
too tricky and suspicious of women to engage in plain
speech without a lot of encouragement. Was she willing
to show him the way? Put her money where her mouth
was? The concept of putting her mouth anywhere near
Navarre was so arousing that she blushed.

Toying with the concept, she went off to shower and
rub scented cream all over her mostly slender body before
applying loads of mascara and lippy. When she saw herself in that exquisite palest green lingerie she almost got
cold feet. The tummy was there, there was no concealing
or avoiding it, but it was his baby and he was definitely
looking forward to its existence, she reminded herself
comfortingly. As long as she wore vertiginous boots and
looked at herself face on rather than taking in her less sensually appealing profile, she decided she didn't look silly.
Donning a black silky raincoat ornamented with lots of
zips that had recently caught her eye for being unusual,
she left the bedroom.

At the airport, Navarre was stunned when, engaged in
commenting on his reorganisation of CCC to a financial
journalist, he glanced across the concourse and saw his
wife awaiting him. That was definitely an unexpected
development. In truth he had been a little edgy about the

latest gift he had sent her. He had worried that it was a step too far, which might upset the marital apple cart even more, and so he had waited until he was out of the country to send it. He could never remember being so unsure with a woman before and he had found it an unnerving experience. As he excused himself to approach her a radiant smile lit up her face and she looked so gorgeous with her spectacular hair tumbling round her fragile features that he almost walked into a woman wheeling a luggage trolley.

'Navarre...' Tawny pronounced, hooking a slender pale hand to his arm.

'I like the coat, *ma petite*,' he murmured, although even with his wide experience he had never before seen a raincoat that appeared to lead a double life as a distinctly sexy garment, for it was short, showing the merest glimpse of long pale thigh and knee above the most incredible pair of long, tight, high-heeled boots.

Luminous pale blue eyes lifted to his face. 'I thought you'd like the boots—'

'*Il n'y a pas de mais*...no buts about that,' Navarre breathed a little thickly, wondering what she was wearing below the coat because from his vantage point no garment was visible at the neck. He watched her climb into the limousine and as the split at the back of the coat parted a tantalising couple of inches along with the movement he froze for a split second at the sight of the pale green knickers riding high on her rounded little bottom.

As the car pulled away, Tawny crossed her legs and asked him about London. His attention was welded to her legs, though, his manner distracted, and when he glanced up to find her watching him, a faint line of colour barred his high cheekbones, highlighting eyes of the most wicked green. 'You have to know that you look amazing,' he stressed unevenly. 'I can't take my eyes off you.'

'That's what I like to hear, but it's been so long since you said anything in that line…or looked,' she pointed out gently.

His lush lashes cloaked his gaze protectively. 'Our wedding day should have been perfect but instead everything went wrong and that was my fault. I didn't feel that I was in a position to make demands. I didn't want to risk driving you away.'

In a sudden movement, Tawny reached for his hand. 'I'm not going anywhere!'

'People said stuff like that to me throughout my childhood and then broke their promises,' he admitted with a stark sincerity that shook her.

'Touching me…I mean,' she said awkwardly, 'it wouldn't have needed a demand.'

Navarre rested a light fingertip below the ripe curve of her raspberry-tinted mouth and said, 'How was I to know that?'

As his hand trailed along her cheekbone Tawny pushed her cheek into his palm, lashes sensually low. 'You know now,' she told him.

'You're so different from the other women I've known. I didn't want to get it wrong with you,' he admitted gruffly, delicious tension stretching out the moment as she angled her mouth up and he took the invitation with a swift, sure hunger that released a moan of approval from her throat.

Navarre straightened again and a gave her a breathtaking smile. 'I dare not touch you until we get back home. I'm like dynamite waiting on a lit match,' he groaned, studying her with hot, hungry intensity. 'It's been too long and I'm too revved up.'

Alight with all the potency of her feminine power, Tawny grinned and whispered curiously, 'How long?'

His brow indented. 'You know how long it's been.'

'You mean…I was your last lover? When we were together that last time in London?' Tawny specified in open amazement. 'There hasn't been anyone else since then?'

Navarre gave a rueful laugh. 'I've always been more into quality than quantity, *chérie*. I'm past the age where I sleep with women purely for kicks.'

Tawny tacitly understood what he was confirming. Even when their short-lived relationship had appeared to be over he had not taken another lover. Obviously he had not met anyone he wanted enough, which with the choices he had to have was a huge compliment to Tawny. Even more obviously, if she accepted his word on that score, it meant that he could not be engaged in even an occasional affair with Tia Castelli. Perhaps he had once loved Tia and although it was in the past, he retained a fondness for the beautiful film star, she reasoned feverishly, desperate to explain what she had seen between them on her wedding day.

But she *was* seriously surprised by the news that he had been celibate for months on end. Meeting his level scrutiny, she believed him on that score one hundred per cent and it was as if the weight of the world fell off her shoulders in the same moment. Suddenly she was furious with herself for not asking questions about Tia and demanding answers sooner. She had conserved her pride and remained silent but unhappy and she wasn't proud of the reality that she had behaved like a coward, frightened of what the truth might reveal and of how much it might hurt. Loving a man who could be so reserved might never be easy, but she needed to learn how to handle that side of his nature.

In the vast bedroom that she had become accustomed to occupying alone she let him unzip the coat and part the edges to look down at her scantily clad curves with smouldering appreciation.

'I'm going to have to start buying you stuff,' she began shyly as he laid her down on the bed and started to carefully unzip her boots.

'No, this moment is my gift,' Navarre countered huskily, burying his mouth between her breasts and running a skilful hand along the extended length of her thigh to the taut triangle of fabric between her legs.

Her body was supersensitive after all the months of deprivation. The pulse of need she was struggling to control tightened up an almost painful notch. Sadly the lingerie that had brought them together received precious little attention and was cast aside within minutes while Navarre's shirt got ripped in the storm of Tawny's impatience. She ran her hands over the gloriously hard, flat expanse of his abs and then lower to the blatant thrust of his arousal. His breath hitched in his throat as he protested that he was too aroused to bear her touch.

'You mean you're only good for one go...like a Christmas cracker?' Tawny asked him deadpan.

And, startled by that teasing analogy, Navarre laughed long and hard as he studied her with fascination. 'Where have you been all my life?'

He kissed her passionately again and matters quickly became extremely heated. He tried to make her wait because he wanted to make an occasion of what he saw as a long delayed wedding night, but she was in no mood for ceremony and she refused to wait, holding him to her with possessive hands and locking her slim legs round his waist to entrap him. She had expectations and she was unusually bossy. He was trying for slow and gentle,

she was striving for hard and fast, and with a little art-
ful angling of her hips and caressing and whispered en-
couragements she got exactly what she wanted delivered
with an unrivalled hunger that left her body singing and
dancing with excitement. Desire momentarily quenched,
she lay in his arms, peacefully enjoying the fact that he
was still touching her as if he couldn't quite believe that
he had now reclaimed that intimacy. He stroked her arm
and strung a line of kisses round the base of her throat
while still holding her close to his lean, damp body and
at that instant, with all that appreciation coming her way,
she felt like a queen.

In fact when he got out of bed she almost panicked, a
small hand clamping round his wrist as if he were a flee-
ing prisoner. 'Where are you going?'

Navarre lifted the phone with a flourish. 'I'm ordering
some food, *ma petite*—we both need sustenance to keep
up the pace.'

'And then?' she checked, heat and awareness still rippling through swollen and sensitive places as she looked
at him.

'We share a shower and I stay…all night?' He was looking hopeful and she knew she wouldn't be able to disap-
point him, particularly when she just didn't want him out
of her sight for a minute.

'And if you should feel the need to wake me up and
jump me during the night at any time,' Navarre drawled
silkily over supper, 'you are very welcome.'

'Well, the pregnancy damage is already done.'

'Don't say that even jokingly,' he urged, feeding her
grapes and Parma ham and tiny sweet tomatoes and reminding her all over again why she loved him so much.
'I can't wait to be a father.'

In the secure circle of Navarre's arms for the first time

ever, Tawny slept blissfully well. To his great disappointment she didn't wake him up for anything so that he could prove all over again that he had nothing in common whatsoever with a Christmas cracker. When she wakened it was late morning and she blinked drowsily. Stretching a hand over to the empty space beside her in the bed, she suppressed a sigh even as she stretched luxuriantly while lazily considering their marriage, which she was finally convinced had a real future. He was gone, of course he was long gone, he left for the office at the crack of dawn most weekdays. Only when she had stumbled out of bed to move in the direction of the bathroom did she realise that Navarre had not even left the room—he was actually seated in an armchair in the dimness.

'My word, I didn't see you over there…what a fright you gave me!' She gasped, stooping hurriedly to pick up her robe from the foot of the bed and dig her arms into the sleeves because she was still somewhat shy of displaying her pregnant body to him. 'Why are you still at home?'

'May I open the curtains?' At her nod, he buzzed back the drapes and light flooded in, illuminating the harsh lines etched in his taut features. 'I've been waiting for you to wake up.'

'What's wrong? What's happened?'

'Your cell phone has been ringing on and off for a couple of hours…your sisters, I assume, your family trying to get in touch with you…I didn't answer the calls.' Navarre lifted a shoulder in a very Gallic shrug and surveyed her with brooding regret. 'I switched off your phone because I wanted to be the one to tell you what has happened—'

'I need to use the bathroom first!' Tawny flung wildly at him and sped in there like a mouse pursued by a cat, slamming the door behind her. She didn't want to know; she didn't want to hear anything bad! She had wakened feeling happy, safe and insanely optimistic for the first time in a long time. How could that precious hope be taken away from her so quickly?

CHAPTER ELEVEN

ONCE Tawny had freshened up and mentally prepared herself for some sort of disaster, she emerged again, pale and tense.

'Has someone died? My gran—?'

'*Merde alors*…no, it is nothing of that nature!' Navarre hastened to assure her.

Tawny breathed again, slow and deep, striving to remain calm when all she really wanted to do was scream and be hysterical and childish because she had never wanted bad news less, and now she feared that he was about to tell her something or *confess* something that would destroy her and their marriage. If nobody had died or got hurt, what else was there?

'I saw Tia while I was over in London. She took a hotel room and I visited her there. Yesterday an English tabloid newspaper published an account of the fact that we were in that hotel suite alone together for more than an hour and printed photos of us entering and leaving the hotel separately.'

Tawny drew her body up so stiff with her muscles pulled so tight that she stretched at least an inch above her normal height. 'You went to an hotel with her…you're admitting that?'

'I won't lie to you about it.'

'You know a normal man would be rendezvousing with his secretary or a colleague between five and seven in the evening for clandestine sex before he comes home to his wife. That's the norm for a mistress—you're not supposed to be shagging a world-famous film star!' Tawny condemned shakily, throwing words in a wild staccato burst while nausea pooled in her stomach because she immediately grasped the appalling fact that his confession meant that all her worst fears were actually true. She felt as if she had woken up inside a nightmare and did not know what to say or do. She hovered on the priceless Aubusson rug, swallowed alive by her anguish.

Navarre was watching every flicker cross her highly expressive face and he too had lost colour below his bronzed complexion. 'Tia is not and has never been my mistress. We're friends and we lunched in her suite in private, that's *all*,' Navarre declared, shifting an emphatic hand to stress that point. 'The paparazzi never leave her alone. Her every move is recorded by cameras. She has to be very careful of her reputation because of her marriage and her career, which is the only reason why we usually meet up in secret—'

'Never mind her. What about *your* marriage?' Tawny asked him baldly, wondering if he could seriously be expecting her to swallow such an unlikely story. Lunch and no sex? What sort of an idiot did he think she was?

A hasty rat-a-tat-tat sounded on the bedroom door and, with a bitten-off curse that betrayed just how worked up he was as well, Navarre strode past her to answer it. Hearing Gaspard's voice, Tawny rested a hand on a corner of the bed and slowly, carefully sank her weak body down on the comfortable mattress. Her legs felt like wet noodles and she felt dizzy and sick. It was nerves and fear, of course, she told herself impatiently. She wasn't about to faint or throw up like some silly Victorian maiden. Her husband had slept with Tia Castelli. In fact he obviously slept with the actress on a very regular basis, for by the sound of it their meeting arrangements seemed to be set in quite a cosy little routine. That suggested that their private encounters had been taking place for at least a couple of years.

Navarre closed the door and raked long restive fingers through his short black hair. Momentarily he closed his eyes as he was struggling to muster his resources.

'What did Gaspard want?'

Navarre expelled his breath in a hiss and shot her a veiled glance. 'To tell me that Tia has arrived—'

'Here? She's *here?*' Tawny exclaimed in utter disbelief.

'We'll talk downstairs and settle this for once and all,' Navarre pronounced grimly. 'I'm sorry I've involved you in this mess—'

'Tia will be even sorrier if I get my hands on her,' Tawny slammed back strickenly. 'How on earth could she come here? What sort of a woman would do that?'

'Think about it,' Navarre urged tautly. 'Only a woman who is not my lover would come to the home I share with my wife—'

'That might be true of most women, but not necessarily when the woman concerned is a drama queen like Tia Castelli! I'll get dressed and come down…but don't you dare go near her without me there!' Tawny warned him fierily while she dug frantically through drawers and wardrobes to gather up an outfit to take into the bathroom.

He's having an affair and his lover has got the brass neck to come to the home he shares with his pregnant wife, she thought in shock and horror. Yet last night they had been so close, so happy together. How could she have been prepared for such a development? In a daze she pulled on her jeans and a loose silk geometric print top. She couldn't even *try* to compete with an international star in the looks department.

He had belonged to Tia first, Tawny reasoned wretchedly, only choosing to marry Tawny because she was pregnant and possibly because he had wanted to make his own life away from Tia's. After all, Tia was married as well. And she could have forgiven him for the affair if he had broken off his liaison with the blonde beauty to concentrate on his marriage instead. But he had not done that. Indeed Navarre appeared to believe that he could somehow have both of them in his life. Did he aspire to enjoying both a mistress *and* a wife?

'What is she doing here in France?' Tawny pressed Navarre on the way downstairs.

'We'll find out soon enough,' Navarre forecast flatly.

A very large set of ornate pale blue leather cases sat in the hall and Tawny was aghast at that less than subtle message. Tia had not only come to visit but also, it seemed, to stay. Tia, sheathed in a black form-fitting dress that hugged her curves, broke into a tumbling flood of Italian as soon as Navarre and Tawny entered the drawing room.

'Speak in English, please,' Navarre urged the overwrought woman. 'Let us be calm.'

Tawny dealt him a pained appraisal. 'Only a man would suggest that in this situation.'

'Luke's thrown me out—he won't listen to anything I say!' Tia cried in English and she threw herself at Navarre like a homing pigeon. 'What am I going to do? What the hell am I going to do now?'

Standing there as superfluous as a third wheel on a bicycle and being totally ignored, Tawny ground her teeth together. 'Well, you *can't* stay here,' she told Tia loudly, reckoning that it would take a raised voice to penetrate the blonde's shell of self-interest.

Slowly, Tia lifted her golden head from Navarre's chest and focused incredulous big blue eyes on Tawny. 'Are you speaking to me?'

'You're not welcome under this roof,' Tawny delivered with quiet dignity.

Ironically, in spite of all that had happened, Tia seemed aghast at that assurance. She backed off a step from Navarre, her full attention locking to him. 'Are you going to allow her to speak to me like that?'

'Tawny is my wife and this is her home. If she doesn't want you staying here in the wake of that scandal in London, which affects me as much as you, I'm afraid you will have to listen to her,' he spelt out.

A little of Tawny's rigid tension eased.

'You should be putting me first—what's the matter with you?' Tia yelled at him accusingly, golden hair bouncing on her shoulders, slender arms spread in dramatic emphasis.

'I'm putting my marriage first but I should have done that sooner,' Navarre murmured levelly and, although he spoke quietly, his deep dark drawl carried. 'Allow me to tell Tawny the truth about our relationship, Tia—'

Tia stalked back towards him, her beautiful face flushed with furious disbelief. 'Absolutely not...you can't tell her...not under *any* circumstances!'

'We don't have a choice,' Navarre declared, his impatience patent while strain and something else Tawny couldn't distinguish warred in his set features as he looked expectantly at the older woman.

Tia shot Tawny a fulminating appraisal. 'Don't tell her. I don't trust her—'

'But I do...' Navarre reached out to Tawny and after

a moment of surprise and hesitation she moved closer to accept his hand and let him draw her beneath one arm. 'Tawny is part of my life now. You can't ignore her, you can't treat her as if she is of no account.'

'If you tell her, if you risk my marriage and my career just to please her, I'll never forgive you for it!' Tia sobbed in a growing rage.

'Your marriage is already at risk but that's not an excuse to put mine in jeopardy as well.' Navarre's arm tightened round Tawny's taut shoulders. 'Tawny...Tia is my mother, but that is a very big secret which you can't share with anyone at all outside this room—'

'Your m-mother?' Tawny stammered, completely disconcerted by that shattering claim and twisting her head to stare at him. 'For goodness' sake, she's not old enough to be your mother!'

Navarre was wryly amused. 'Tia is a good deal older than she looks.'

Tia went rigid with resentment at that statement. 'I was only a child when I gave birth to you—'

'She was twenty-one but pretending to be a teenager at the time,' Navarre extended wearily. 'I'll tell you the rest of the story some other time but right now the fact that she is my mother and that we like to stay in regular contact is really all that's relevant.'

'His...mother,' Tawny framed weakly, still studying the glamorous older woman in disbelief, for, according to what Navarre had just told her, Tia had to be into her fifties yet she could still comfortably pass for being a woman in her late thirties. Shock was still gripping Tawny so hard that she could hardly think straight.

'But that can never come out in public,' Tia proclaimed, angrily defensive. 'I've told lies. I've kept secrets. It would destroy my reputation and I don't want Luke to know that his own mother is younger than I am—'

'I bet she's not a beauty like you, though,' Tawny commented thoughtfully and earned an almost appreciative glance from the woman whom she had just discovered to be her mother-in-law.

'I think Luke could adapt,' Navarre interposed soothingly. 'You're still the same woman he loved and married.'

Tia shuddered. 'He would never forgive me for lying to him.'

'Why were you crying on our wedding day?' Tawny enquired to combat the simple fact that she was still dizzily thinking, She can't be his mother, she *can't* be!

'Do I *look* like I want to be a grandmother?' Tia demanded in a tone of horror. 'Do I look that old?'

'I don't think you'll ever be asked to carry out that role,' Tawny responded drily, weary of the woman's enormous vanity and concern about her age while she instinctively continued to study those famous features in search of a likeness between mother and son. And she realised that when she removed their very different colouring from the comparison there was quite a definite similarity in bone structure. He was so good-looking because his mother was gorgeous, she registered numbly.

'Right now I only want to lie down and rest. I'm exhausted,' Tia complained petulantly, treating both her son and his wife to an accusing look as though that were their fault. 'I assume I can stay now that I've shown my credentials.'

'Yes, of course,' Tawny confirmed, marvelling that such a selfish personality had ever contrived to win Navarre's loyalty and tenderness. And yet, without a shadow of a doubt, Tia had. Tawny had not been mistaken over what she had thought she had seen in Navarre when he was with his mother on their wedding day. He cared for the volatile woman.

'If you want to sort this out with Luke you will have to let him into the secret,' Navarre warned his mother levelly.

Tia told him to mind his own business with a tartness that was very maternal, but which would have been more suited to a little boy than an adult male. Gaspard was summoned to show Tia to her room. Tawny had offered but was imperiously waved away, Tia clearly not yet prepared to accept a friendly gesture from her corner. Tawny grasped that she had a possessive mother-in-law to deal with, for Tia undoubtedly resented Navarre's loyalty to his wife.

Tia swept out and the door closed. Navarre looked at Tawny.

Tawny winced and said limply, 'Wow, your mother's quite a character.'

'She's temperamental when she gets upset. I wanted to tell you but a long time ago I swore never to tell anyone that I was her son and she held me to my promise.'

'Your mother...' Tawny shook her head very slowly. 'I never would have guessed that in a million years.'

Over breakfast and only after Tawny had phoned her sisters to tell them that, *no,* she really wasn't concerned about silly stories in the papers, Navarre explained the intricacies of his birth, which had been buried deep and concealed behind a wall of lies to protect Tia's star power. According to Tia's official history she had been discovered as a fifteen year old schoolgirl in the street by a famous director. Her first film had won so many awards it had gone global and shot her to stardom. In fact the pretence that she was much younger had simply been a publicity exercise and her kid sister's birth certificate had been used for proof when Tia was actually twenty-one years old. Soon after her discovery she had fallen pregnant by the famous director. A scandalous affair with a married man threatened to destroy her pristine reputation and her embryo career, so Navarre's birth had taken place in secrecy. Tia had travelled to Paris with her older sister and had pretended to be her so that her baby could be registered as her sister's child. That cover up achieved, Tia had returned to show business while paying her sister and her boyfriend to raise Navarre in a Paris flat.

Tawny was frowning. 'Then how come you ended up in foster care?'

'I have no memory of my aunt at all. She only kept me for a couple of years. The money Tia used to buy her sister's silence was spent on drugs and when my aunt died of an overdose I joined the care system. I had no idea I had a mother alive until I was eighteen and at university,' Navarre extended wryly. 'I was approached by a lawyer first, carefully sworn to silence—'

'And then you met your mother. Must've been a shock,' Tia remarked.

An almost boyish expression briefly crossed his lean taut face as he looked back into the past and his handsome mouth took on a wry cast. 'I was in complete awe of her.'

Tawny could hardly imagine the full effect of Tia Castelli on a teenager who had been totally alone in the world all his life. Naturally his mother had walked straight into his heart when he had never had anyone of his own before. 'She's very beautiful.'

'Tia may not be showing it right now but she does also have tremendous charm. Ever since then we've been meeting up at least once a month and we often talk on the phone and email. That's one of the reasons I was so concerned that someone might have accessed my laptop,' he confided. 'I've seen her through many, many crises and have become her rock in every storm. I'm very fond of her.'

Tawny nodded. 'Even though she won't own up to you in public?'

'What would that mean to me at my age? I know she's far from perfect,' Navarre acknowledged with a dismissive lift of an ebony brow. 'But what else does she know? She was an abused child from a very poor home.'

Tawny was not as understanding of his mother's flaws as he was. 'But what did she ever do for you? You had a miserable childhood.'

'But it made me strong, *chérie*. As for Tia, even after decades of fame she still lives in terror of losing everything she has. She did what she thought best for me at the time. She helped me find my first job, invested in my first company, undoubtedly helped me to become the success that I am today.'

'That's just the power of money you're talking about and I doubt if it meant much to someone as rich as she must be.' Her eyes glittered silver with moisture, the tightening of her throat muscles as she fought back tears lending her voice a hoarse edge. 'I'm thinking of the child you were, growing up without a mother or love or anyone of your own…I can't bear the thought of that.'

In an abrupt movement that lacked his normal measured grace, Navarre vaulted upright and walked round the table to lift Tawny up out of her seat. *'Je vais bien…* I'm OK. But I admit that I didn't know what love was until I met you.'

Assuming that he had guessed how she felt about him, Tawny reddened. 'Am I that obvious?'

A gentle fingertip traced the silvery trail of a tear on her cheek.

'There is nothing obvious about you. In fact you de-ied my understanding from the first moment we met and, he more I saw of you, the more desperately I wanted to know what it was about you which got to me when other women never had.'

Her lashes flicked up on curious eyes. 'I…got to you? In what way?'

'In every way a woman can appeal to a man. First to my body, then to my brain and finally to my heart,' Navarre specified. 'And you dug in so deep in my heart, I was wretched without you when we were apart but far too proud to come looking for you again.'

Tawny rested a hand on a broad shoulder to steady her-self. 'Wretched?' she repeated doubtfully, unable to asso-ciate such a word with him.

A rueful smile shadowed Navarre's wide eloquent mouth. 'I was very unhappy and unsettled for weeks on end. I thought I was infatuated with you. I tried so hard to fight it and forget about you but it didn't work.'

'Navarre…' Tawny breathed uncertainly. 'Are you try-ing to tell me that you love me?'

'Obviously not doing a very good job of it. I think it was love at first sight.' His eyes gazed down into hers full of warmth and tenderness. 'I've been in love with you for months. I knew I loved you long before I married you. Why do you think I was so keen to put that wedding ring on your hand?'

'The b-baby.'

Navarre drew her back against him and splayed a pos-sessive hand across the firm swell of her stomach. 'I have very good intentions towards our baby but I married you because I loved you and wanted to share my life with you, c'est ce pas?'

'But you said you were strongly attracted to me and that that was enough.'

'I said what I had to say to get that ring on your finger for real,' Navarre breathed, pressing his mouth to the sensitive nape of her neck and making her shiver with sudden awareness. 'I'm a ruthless man. I would have said whatever it took to achieve that goal because I believed the end result would be worth it. I was determined that you would be mine for ever, *ma petite*.'

Overjoyed by that admission, Tawny twisted round and pressed her hands to his strong cheekbones to align their mouths and kiss him with slow, sweet brevity as more questions that had to be answered bubbled up in her brain. 'What on earth was on that laptop of yours?'

'CCC buyout stuff and some very personal emails from Tia. She tells me everything.'

'No wonder Luke's jealous of you.'

'As long as Tia refuses to tell him the truth I am powerless to alter that situation.'

Tawny treated him to a shrewd appraisal. 'She's part of the reason you wanted a fake fiancée for the Golden Awards, isn't she?'

'I promised Tia that I would bring a girlfriend and too believed it to be a sensible precaution where Luke was concerned. Unfortunately the lady backed out at the last minute and—'

'And you hired me instead,' Tawny slotted in. 'What happened to the lady who backed out?'

'I told her that I'd met someone else when I got back to Paris.'

'But that wasn't true…you had already left me.'

His eyes glimmered. 'But I still didn't want anyone else. You had me on a chain by then. Don't you remember that last night in London when I came to your door?'

Tawny stiffened. 'I also recall how it ended with you telling me I was a good—'

Navarre pulled her up against him and gazed down at her in reproof. 'Wasn't that in response to you threatening to tell the world what I was like in bed?'

A sensual shimmer of response wafted through Tawny and she pressed closer, tucking her head into his shoulder to breathe in the deliriously addictive scent of his skin. 'Well, now that you mention it, it might have been,' she teased, acknowledging that she had met her match while relishing the claim she had had him on a chain by that stage. A chain of love and commitment he refused to give to a woman who was a failed thief threating to tell all to the newspapers? She didn't blame him for that, she couldn't blame him for walking away at that point, for one thing she did appreciate about the man she loved was his very strong moral compass.

'When I saw you with Tia at the wedding I feared the worst,' she confided as his arms tightened round her.

'I was desperate to tell you the truth and relieved when you didn't force a scene because I didn't want to break my promise to my mother,' he admitted grimly. 'But I should have broken the promise and told you then. Unfortunately it took me a few weeks to appreciate that as my wife you have to have the strongest claim to my loyalty.'

'Sorry about the wedding night that never was,' she mumbled ruefully. 'I felt so insecure after seeing how close you were to her. I could *see* that there was a connection between you and I love you so much...'

Navarre pushed up her chin and stared down at her searchingly. 'Since when?' he demanded and his beautiful mouth quirked. 'Since you saw my beautiful castle in France?'

His wife dealt him a reproving look. 'I shall treat that

suggestion with the contempt it deserves! No, I fell for
you long before that. Remember that breakfast in Scotland
after that nasty newspaper spread which revealed that I
was a maid? When you brought me my food and stood by
me in front of everyone as though nothing had happened
I really *loved* you for it…'

'Snap. I loved you for your dignity and cool, *ma petite*.'
A tender smile softened the often hard line of his shapely
mouth. Long fingers stroked her spine as he crushed her
to him and kissed her with a breathless hunger that made
her knees weak.

For once, Tawny had a small breakfast because the conversation and what followed were too entertaining to take
a rain check on. He urged her upstairs to the bed they had
only shared once and they lost themselves in the passion
they had both restrained for so long.

In the lazy aftermath of quenching their desire, Tawny
stared at her handsome husband and said, 'What on earth
game have you been playing with me all these week
we've been married?'

'It was no game.' Navarre laughed. 'We had no court-
ship—we never dated. I was trying to go back to the beginning and do everything differently in the hope that you
would start feeling for me what I felt for you.'

In dismay at that simple exclamation and touched that
he had gone to that amount of idealistic effort without
receiving the appreciation he had undoubtedly deserved,
Tawny clamped a hand to her lips. 'Oh, my goodness, how
stupid am I that I didn't see that?'

Navarre looked a touch superior and stretched luxuriantly against the tumbled sheets while regarding her with
intense appreciation. 'Of the two of us, I'm the romantic
one. Don't forget that reality when you next draw a cartoon
in which I figure merely as a skirt-chasing Frenchman!'

Tawny smoothed a possessive hand over his spectacu-lar abs and smiled down at him with unusual humility. 'I won't,' she promised happily. 'I love you just the way you are.'

EPILOGUE

JOIE, named for the joy she had brought her adoring parents, toddled across the floor and presented Luke Conver with a toy brick.

'She's cute but I wouldn't want one of my own,' the roc musician said with an apologetic grimace as he droppe down on his knees to place the brick where Navarre an Tawny's daughter, with her fantastically curly black hai and pale blue eyes, wanted it placed. 'I grew up the young est of nine kids and I've never wanted that kind of hassl for myself.'

'Kids aren't for everyone,' Tawny agreed, thinkin of how much her mother had resented being a paren yet Susan Baxter had proved to be a much more inter ested grandmother than her daughter had expected. I fact mother and daughter had become a good deal close since Joie's birth in London eighteen months earlier.

Tawny often spent weekends in London to meet up wit her sisters and her mother before travelling down to se her grandmother. She had been married to Navarre for tw years and had never been happier or more content. Sh and Navarre seemed to fit like two halves of a whole. He liveliness had lightened his character and brought out h sense of humour, while his cooler reserve had quietene her down just a tiny bit. Through her cartoons, Tawn

d become quite a familiar face in Parisian society, and
hen 'The English Wife' cartoons had run out of steam
e had come up with a cartoon strip based on an average
mily, which had done even more for her career.

A peal of laughter sounded in the hall of Navarre and
wny's spacious London home followed by an animated
rst of Italian, and Luke grinned and sprang upright.
ia's back...'

Tawny's mother-in-law, swathed in a spectacular crim-
n dress and looking ravishingly beautiful, posed like the
ollywood star she was in the doorway, and her husband
inned and pulled her into his arms with scant concern
r their audience. Within the space of thirty seconds they
d vanished upstairs. Tia had just finished filming in
oatia and Luke was about to set off on tour round the
SA. As they had been apart for weeks and Luke had a
pover in the city Tia had invited herself and her hus-
nd to dinner and to spend the night.

From the moment that Tia had finally faced reality and
rsuaded Navarre to take care of the challenging task of
ling Luke who he really was, all unease between the
o couples had vanished. Luke had been very shocked,
t relieved by the news that he had no reason to feel
eatened by Navarre's bond with Tia, and certainly the
elation did not seem to have dented Luke's devotion
his demanding wife. Navarre would be Tia's big dark
ret until the day he died but that didn't bother him and
he paparazzi were still chasing around trying to make
candal out of his encounters with his mother, it no lon-
worried him or her. The people that mattered knew
truth and Navarre had no further need to keep secrets
m Tawny.

Tia was a fairly uninterested grandmother, freezing
h dismay if Joie and her not always perfectly clean

hands got too close to her finery. Tia's life revolved roun
her latest movie, her most recent reviews and Luke, who
she uncritically adored. She had initially taken a step ba
from her son but that hadn't lasted for long, Tawny thoug
wryly, for Tia rejoiced in a strong manly shoulder to le
on and Navarre was very good at fulfilling that role wh
Luke was unavailable. Tia's marriage had become rath
more stable and fortunately the passionate disputes h
died down a little, so Navarre was much less in dema
in that field. Tawny, who had nursed certain fears, al
had to admit that Tia never interfered as a mother-in-la
She had become friendlier, but at heart Tia Castelli wou
always be a larger-than-life star and she didn't really 'c
normal family relationships or even understand them.

Navarre, who had flown Tia back from Europe in l
private jet, appeared in the doorway.

'Where have our guests gone?' Tawny's tall, dark
handsome husband enquired, bending down to scoop
the toddler shouting with excitement at his appearanc

Tawny watched with amusement as Navarre's imma
late appearance was destroyed by his daughter's enthu
astic welcome. His black hair was ruffled, his tie yank
and he was almost strangled by the little arms tighteni
round his neck, but he handled his livewire child with l
ing amusement.

'Our guests are staging their reunion...we just may f
ourselves dining alone tonight,' Tawny warned him,
easy smile illuminating her face.

'That would be perfect,' Navarre confided as he
Joie down to run to her nanny, who had appeared in
hall. *'Merci,* Antoinette.'

'I don't really want company either when you've b
away for a couple of days,' Navarre admitted bluntly o

he door closed on their nanny's exit with their daughter. Whose idea was this set-up anyway?'

'You need to ask? Tia's, of course. You're so posses-ive, Monsieur Cazier,' Tawny teased, but when those in-ent green eyes looked at her like that she knew she was oved and she adored that sensation of warm acceptance.

'And with you getting more beautiful every day that's ot going to change any time soon, *ma petite*.'

'How do I know you haven't simply become less picky ince you met me?' Tawny teased.

'Because every month that I have you and Joie in my fe I love you even more,' he murmured with roughened incerity as he drew her into his arms. 'My life would be o empty, so bleak without you both.'

'I missed you,' she admitted in reward.

'So much,' Navarre growled, leaning in for a hungry, emanding kiss. 'What time's dinner?'

'I thought, since our guests have made themselves carce, we could go out…later,' Tawny whispered en-ouragingly.

'This is why I love you so much,' Navarre swore with assionate admiration. 'You've worked out what I want efore I even speak.'

Tawny knotted his tie in one hand and laughed. 'And metimes I even give you what you want because I love ou…'

'And I love you,' Navarre husked, making no attempt conceal his appreciation.

* * * * *

CLASSIC

COMING NEXT MONTH from Harlequin Presents®
AVAILABLE JUNE 26, 2012

#3071 HEART OF A DESERT WARRIOR
Lucy Monroe
Sheikh Asad needs to secure his legacy, and Iris is the key.
Can she resist so determined a seduction?

#3072 SANTINA'S SCANDALOUS PRINCESS
The Santina Crown
Kate Hewitt
Pampered princess Natalia has swapped couture and
cocktails for photocopying! How long will she last working
for the devilishly handsome Ben Jackson?

#3073 DEFYING DRAKON
The Lyonedes Legacy
Carole Mortimer
Drakon Lyonedes has power, wealth, sex appeal...and any
woman he wants! Until beautiful Gemini Bartholomew enters
his life, that is...

#3074 CAPTIVE BUT FORBIDDEN
Lynn Raye Harris
Bodyguard Rajesh Vala must protect Veronica—whatever the
cost.... But Veronica has always rebelled against commands
and isn't making Raj's job easy!

#3075 HIS MAJESTY'S MISTAKE
A Royal Scandal
Jane Porter
Princess Emmeline is everything this desert king shouldn't
want... Posing as her twin sister and Makin's secretary, she's
playing with fire!

#3076 THE DARK SIDE OF DESIRE
Julia James
Business legend Leon Marantz exudes a dark power that
sends shivers through Flavia Lassiter's body—threatening to
shatter the icy shell protecting her heart.

You can find more information on upcoming Harlequin®
titles, free excerpts and more at www.Harlequin.com.

HPCNM06

REQUEST YOUR FREE BOOKS!

◆Harlequin *Presents*

**2 FREE NOVELS PLUS
2 FREE GIFTS!**

PASSION GUARANTEED SEDUCTION

YES! Please send me 2 FREE Harlequin Presents® novels and my 2 FREE gifts (gifts are worth about \$10). After receiving them, if I don't wish to receive any more books, I can return the shipping statement marked "cancel." If I don't cancel, I will receive 6 brand-new novels every month and be billed just \$4.30 per book in the U.S. or \$4.99 per book in Canada. That's a saving of at least 14% off the cover price! It's quite a bargain! Shipping and handling is just 50¢ per book in the U.S. and 75¢ per book in Canada.* I understand that accepting the 2 free books and gifts places me under no obligation to buy anything. I can always return a shipment and cancel at any time. Even if I never buy another book, the two free books and gifts are mine to keep forever.

106/306 HDN FERQ

Name	(PLEASE PRINT)	
Address		Apt. #
City	State/Prov.	Zip/Postal Code

Signature (if under 18, a parent or guardian must sign)

Mail to the **Reader Service:**
IN U.S.A.: P.O. Box 1867, Buffalo, NY 14240-1867
IN CANADA: P.O. Box 609, Fort Erie, Ontario L2A 5X3

Not valid for current subscribers to Harlequin Presents books.

**Are you a current subscriber to Harlequin Presents books
and want to receive the larger-print edition?
Call 1-800-873-8635 or visit www.ReaderService.com.**

* Terms and prices subject to change without notice. Prices do not include applicable taxes. Sales tax applicable in N.Y. Canadian residents will be charged applicable taxes. Offer not valid in Quebec. This offer is limited to one order per household. All orders subject to credit approval. Credit or debit balances in a customer's account(s) may be offset by any other outstanding balance owed by or to the customer. Please allow 4 to 6 weeks for delivery. Offer available while quantities last.

Your Privacy—The Reader Service is committed to protecting your privacy. Our Privacy Policy is available online at www.ReaderService.com or upon request from the Reader Service.

We make a portion of our mailing list available to reputable third parties that offer products we believe may interest you. If you prefer that we not exchange your name with third parties, or if you wish to clarify or modify your communication preferences, please visit us at www.ReaderService.com/consumerschoice or write to us at Reader Service Preference Service, P.O. Box 9062, Buffalo, NY 14269. Include your complete name and address.

*Patricia Thayer welcomes you to Larkville, Texas,
in THE COWBOY COMES HOME—book 1 in the exciting
new 8-book miniseries, THE LARKVILLE LEGACY,
from Harlequin® Romance.*

REACHING THE BANK, Jess climbed down, smiling as she
walked her mount to the water. "Wow, I haven't ridden like
that in years."

"You're good."

"I'm Clay Calhoun's daughter. I'm supposed to be a
good rider."

"You miss him."

She walked with him through the stiff winter grass to
the tree. "It's hard to imagine the Double Bar C going on
without him. He loved this land." She glanced around the
landscape. "Now my brother runs the operation, but he'll be
gone awhile." She released a breath. "I have to say we miss
his leadership."

He frowned. "Is there anything I can do?"

"Thank you. You're handling Storm—that's a big enough
help. It's just that it would be nice to have my brothers and
sister here." She looked at him. "Do you have any siblings?"

He shook his head. "None that I know of."

"What about your father?" she asked.

He shook his head. "Never been in my life. I tried for years
to track him down, but I never could catch up with him."

He caught the sadness etched on her face. "Johnny, I'm
sorry."

He hated pity, especially from her. "Why? You had
nothing to do with it. Jake Jameson didn't want to be found,
to meet his son." He shrugged. "You can't miss what you've
never had. I'm not much of a homebody, either. I guess

that's why I like to keep moving."

Jess looked out over the land. "I guess that's where we're different. I've never really moved away from Larkville."

"Why should you want to leave? You have your business here and your home."

She smiled. "I had to fight Dad to live on my own. But I've got a little Calhoun stubbornness, too."

"You got all the beauty."

Johnny came closer, removed her hat and studied her face. "Your eyes are incredible. And your mouth… I could kiss you for hours."

She sucked in a breath and raised her gaze to his. "Johnny… We weren't going to start this."

"Don't look now, darlin', but it's already started."

Find out what happens between Johnny and Jess in
THE COWBOY COMES HOME by Patricia Thayer,
available July 2012!

And find out how Jess's family will be transformed
in the 8-book series:
THE LARKVILLE LEGACY
A secret letter…two families changed forever

This summer, celebrate everything Western
with Harlequin® Books!

www.Harlequin.com/Western

Harlequin® Romance

THE LARKVILLE LEGACY

A secret letter...two families changed forever

Welcome to Larkville, Texas, where the Calhoun family has
been ranching for generations. When Jess Calhoun discovers
a secret, unopened letter written to her late father, she learns
that there is a whole other branch of her family. Find out
what happens when the two sides meet....

**A new Larkville Legacy story is available every
month beginning July 2012.**

Collect all 8 tales!

Harlequin® Romance

*Three billionaire brothers. Three guarded hearts.
Three fabulous stories.*

SHIRLEY JUMP

*begins a new miniseries that is sure
to capture your heart.*

The McKENNA BROTHERS

When self-made millionaire and CEO Finn McKenna finds his
business in trouble due to a very public scandal, he turns to business
rival Ellie Winston for help. But Ellie wants a different kind
of merger—marriage!

ONE DAY TO FIND A HUSBAND
Available in July

And coming soon!

HOW THE PLAYBOY GOT SERIOUS
Riley McKenna's story, available in August

THE RETURN OF THE LAST McKENNA
Brody McKenna's story, available in September

Available wherever books are sold.